The Hallowed Isle

Book Four:

The Book of the Stone

The Hallowed Isle *cycle by*
Diana L. Paxson

The Book of the Sword
The Book of the Spear
The Book of the Cauldron
The Book of the Stone

Wodan's Children *Trilogy*

The Dragons of the Rhine
The Wolf and the Raven
The Lord of Horses

With Adrienne Martine-Barnes

Master of Earth and Water
The Shield Between the Worlds
Sword of Fire and Shadow

THE HALLOWED ISLE

BOOK FOUR:
THE BOOK OF THE STONE

DIANA L. PAXSON

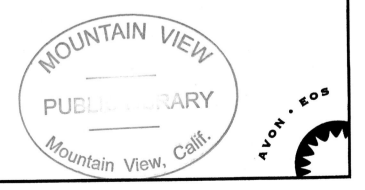

AVON · EOS

This is a work of fiction. Names, characters, places, and incidents either are the product of the author's imagination or are used fictitiously. Any resemblance to actual events, locales, organizations, or persons, living or dead, is entirely coincidental and beyond the intent of either the author or the publisher.

AVON BOOKS, INC.
1350 Avenue of the Americas
New York, New York 10019

Copyright © 2000 by Diana L. Paxson
Cover illustration and design by Tom Canty
Interior design by Kellan Peck
Published by arrangement with the author
ISBN: 0-380-80548-0
www.avonbooks.com/eos

Library of Congress Cataloging in Publication Data:

Paxson, Diana L.
    The book of the stone / Diana L. Paxson.
        p.   cm. — (The hallowed isle : bk. 4)
    1. Great Britain—History—Anglo Saxon period. 449-1066 Fiction.   2. Arthurian romances Adaptations.   3. Arthur, King Fiction.   I. Title.   II. Series: Paxson, Diana L. Hallowed isle : bk. 4.
    PS3566.A897B664   2000   99-39528
    813'.54—dc21   CIP

First Avon Eos Printing: January 2000

AVON EOS TRADEMARK REG. U.S. PAT. OFF. AND IN OTHER COUNTRIES, MARCA REGISTRADA, HECHO EN U.S.A.

Printed in the U.S.A.

OPM   10   9   8   7   6   5   4   3   2   1

In Memoriam
Paul Edwin Zimmer

ACKNOWLEDGMENTS

To do justice to my sources for Hallowed Isle would require a bibliography the size of a chapter. These are only some of the materials which have been most useful.

First and foremost, *The Age of Arthur* by John Morris, recently reprinted by Barnes and Noble. This is the best historical overview of the Arthurian period, and with a few exceptions, I have adopted his dates for events.

For names and places, *Roman Britain*, by Plantagenet Somerset Fry, also published by Barnes and Noble; and the British Ordnance Survey maps of Roman Britain and Britain in the Dark Ages.

For fauna and flora, the Country Life book of *The Natural History of the British Isles*.

The History of the Kings of Britain, by Geoffrey of Monmouth, with an occasional glance at Malory's *Morte D'Arthur.*

For the history of the North, *Scotland Before History,* by Stuart Piggott, and W. A. Cummings' *The Age of the Picts.*

For the Anglo-Saxons, the fine series of booklets published by Anglo-Saxon Books, 25 Malpas Dr., Pinner, Middlesex, England.

For insight and inspiration, *Ladies of the Lake,* by John and Caitlin Matthews, and *Merlin through the Ages,* edited by R. J. Stewart and John Matthews.

And a great many maps, local guidebooks, and booklets on regional folklore.

My special thanks to Heather Rose Jones, for her Welsh name lists and instruction on the mysteries of fifth-century. British spelling, and to Winifred Hodge for checking my Old English.

Through the fields of European literature, the Matter of Britain flows as a broad and noble stream. I offer this tributary with thanks and recognition to all those who have gone before.

Feast of Brigid, 1999

CONTENTS

The Hallowed Isle

Book Four:
The Book of the Stone

PROLOGVE

*E*ARTH IS THE MOTHER OF US ALL, AND THE BONES OF OF THE *earth are made of stone. Stone is the foundation of the world.*

Born from fire, stone heaves skyward, taking a thousand forms. Cooling and coalescing, it endures the wearing of water, the rasp of the wind, becomes soil from which living things can grow. The earth convulses, burying the soil, and pressure compresses it into rock once more. As age follows age, the cycle repeats, preserving the bones of plant and animal in eternal stone. The lives of her creatures are but instants in the ages of the earth, but the stone preserves their memories.

Stone is the historian of humanity. The first primates to know themselves as men make from stone the tools that carry their identity. Time passes and the ice comes and goes again. Humans cut wood with tools of stone and build houses, till the soil and form communities. Laboring together, they drag great stones across the land, raise menhirs and barrows, great henges to chart the movements of the stars, and grave them with the spiral patterns of power.

With boundary stones the tribes mark off their territories, but in the center of each land lies the omphalos, *the navel stone, the sacred center of their world. When the destined king sets foot upon it, the stone sings in triumphant vindication for those who have ears to hear.*

But kings die, and one tribe gives way to another on the land. The makers of the henges pass away, and only their stones remember them. Wise Druids incorporate them into their own mysteries. The men of the Eagles net the land with straight tracks of stone, and around the king stones the grass grows high. But the earth turns, and in time the Romans, too, are gone.

But stone endures.

The bones of the earth uphold the world. In the stones of the earth, all that has been lives still in memory.

THE SEED ONCE SOWN

A.D. 502

THE BONES OF THE EARTH WERE CLOSE TO THE SURFACE HERE.
Artor let the horse he was leading halt and gazed around
him at grey stone scoured bare by the storms, furred here and
there by a thin pelt of grass where seeds had rooted themselves in pockets of soil. Harsh though they were, the mountains where once the Silure tribesmen had roamed had their
own uncompromising beauty, but they had little mercy for
those footed creatures that dared to search out their mysteries. Sheepherds followed their sheep across these hills, but
even they rarely climbed so high.

The black horse, finding the grass too short and thin to be
worth grazing, butted Artor gently and the high king took a
step forward. In the clear light Raven's coat gleamed like the
wing of the bird that had given him his name. The stallion
had gone lame a little past mid-morning. The stag they were
trailing was long gone, and the rest of the hunters after it.
The track that Artor was following now, though it crested the
ridge before descending into the valley, was the shortest way
home.

A stone turned beneath his foot and he tensed against remembered pain. But his muscles, warmed by the exercise,

3

flexed and held without a twinge. Indeed, at forty-two, he was as hale and strong as he had ever been. And Britannia was at peace after untold years of war.

It still seemed strange to him to contemplate a year without a campaign. He would have to think of something—public works, perhaps—on which his chieftains could spend their energy so they did not begin fighting one another. He had even begun to hope that he might find it in him to be a true husband to Guendivar.

Artor was still not quite accustomed to being able to move freely—for three years the wound that Melwas' spear had torn through his groin had pained him. The night when the Cauldron, borne through the hall of Camalot by invisible hands, had healed them all was scarcely three months ago.

And a good thing, too—half lamed, he could never have made this climb under his own power. But, now, gazing out across a landscape of blue distances ribbed by ridge and valley, the king blessed the mischance that had brought him here. On the Sunday past, Father Paternus had preached about the temptation of Christ, whom the Devil had carried off to a high place to show him all the kingdoms of the world and their glory. Looking around him, Artor thought that the writer of the gospel must have gotten it wrong somehow, for he himself was high king of all he could see, and the sight of it did not fill him with pride and power, but with wonder.

And, he thought as the next moment brought new awareness, with humility. How could any man look upon this mighty expanse of plain and mountain and say he ruled it all?

Below him the land fell away in long green slopes towards the estuary of the Sabrina, touched here and there with the gold of turning leaves. A smudge of smoke dimmed the tiled roofs of Castra Legionis; beyond them he could just make out the blue gleam of the Sabrina itself. Closer still he glimpsed the villa from which the hunting party had set out that morning. To the south across the water stretched the dim blur of the Dumnonian lands. Eastward lay the midlands, and beyond them Londinium and the Saxon territories. Looking north he could imagine the whole length of the island, all the way to the Alban tribes beyond the Wall. The sky to the north was curdled with clouds. A storm was coming, but he had a little time before it was here.

From this mountaintop, the works of humankind were no more than smudges upon the hallowed isle of Britannia, set like a jewel in the shining silver of the sea.

But it does not belong to me— Artor thought then. *Better to say that I belong to the land.*

A nudge from Raven brought him back from his reverie and he grinned, turning to rub the horse behind his swiveling ears, where the black hide sweated beneath the bridle. Men were not made to live on such heights, and at this time of year darkness would be gathering before he reached shelter. He patted the black's neck, took up the reins, and started down the hill.

For years, thought Medraut, these hills had haunted his dreams. But he had not visited the Isle of Maidens since his childhood, and he had convinced himself that the dark and looming shapes he remembered were no more than a child's imaginings. He was accustomed to mountains—the high, wild hills of the Pictish country, and the tangled hills of the Votadini lands. Why should these be so different? But with every hour he rode, the humped shapes grew closer, and more terrible.

They are my mother's hills . . . he thought grimly. *They are like her.* As he dreaded these hills, he dreaded the thought of confronting her. But he was fifteen, and a man. Neither fear could stop him now.

At Voreda he found a shepherd who agreed to guide him in exchange for a few pieces of gold. For three days they followed the narrow trail that led through the high meadows and down among the trees. Like many men who have lived much alone, the shepherd was inclined to chatter when in company, and gabbled cheerfully until a glare from Medraut stopped him. After that, they rode in a gloomy silence that preyed upon the young man's nerves until he was almost ready to order the shepherd to start talking again.

But by then they had reached the pass below the circle of

stones, and Medraut could see the Lake, and the round island, and the thatched roofs of buildings gleaming through its trees. He paid the shepherd then and sent him away, saying that from here he could follow the trail to the coast without a guide. He did not particularly care if the old man believed him, as long as he went away. The remainder of this journey must be accomplished alone.

To be alone was frightening, but it carried with it the heady taste of freedom. Throughout the years of his growing, his mother had always been present even when she was not physically there, as if the belly cord still connected them. And then, three months ago, when the full moon hung in the sky, the link had disappeared.

For weeks he had been half paralyzed with terror, expecting every messenger to tell them that Morgause was dead. It was Cunobelinus, riding through the great gates with his men behind him, who informed Medraut that his mother was at the Lake with the priestesses of the Isle of Maidens, and that from now on Cunobelinus himself would serve as regent as well as warleader for the northern Votadini, and rule from Dun Eidyn.

The new regent was civil, and his people treated Medraut as a royal prince when they had time to notice him at all. It was not loss of status that had sent him southward. It was the thing he had learned while he still feared Morgause dead that burned in his belly and had driven him here to confront her. It was hard to admit anger when one was torn by the grief of loss. But his mother was still alive.

Medraut was free to hate her now.

"What are you doing here?"

Medraut spun around, for a moment too astonished not to have sensed that his mother had entered the small, white-washed chamber where the priestesses had placed him to answer her. Tuned since birth to her presence, he should have vibrated like a harpstring when its octave is plucked. But the link between them was broken; if he had doubted, he felt the truth of that now.

"Without a word, you abandoned me. Is it so surprising I should come to see how you fared?"

Morgause eyed him uncertainly. Clearly she too felt the difference in the energy between them, all the more, he reflected angrily, because she had not been expecting it. Obviously she had not known their bond was broken. Since she went away she had not thought about him at all.

"As you see," she said finally, "I am well."

His eyes narrowed. "You are changed." And indeed it was so, though at first glance it was hard to describe what had altered. Where before she had always worn black and crimson, now she was dressed in the dark blue of a senior priestess on the Isle. But that was only external. Perhaps it was the fact that her high color had faded that made her seem different, or the new silver in her hair. Or perhaps it was the aura of power, almost of violence, that had always surrounded her, that was gone.

Medraut probed with his inner senses, as she had taught him, and recoiled, blinking. The power was still there, but leashed and contained. It occurred to him that her inner stillness might, if anything, make her stronger. A frightening thought, but it would make no difference, he reminded himself. After today nothing she did could hurt him anymore.

His mother's shoulders twitched in a shrug—a subtle, complex movement that simultaneously suggested apology, pride, and oddly, laughter. She looked at him directly then, and he shivered.

"So are you." Her voice was without expression. She asked again, "Why did you come?"

"To accuse you—" The words came out in a whisper, and Medraut cleared his throat angrily. "You killed her. Without a word to me. You had Kea murdered! Why?!"

He had expected disdain or anger, but not the flat incomprehension with which Morgause gazed back at him.

"The slave girl!" he said desperately. "The one I slept with at Fodreu!" How inadequate those words were for what Kea had done for him, making of her forced choice a gift that transformed him, as if by receiving his first seed, she had given birth to him as a man.

For a moment her eyes flashed in the way he remembered, then she sighed. "Did you love her? I am sorry."

He cleared his throat. "Sorry that I loved her, or that you had her put down like a sick dog?"

"At the time . . . it seemed best to ensure that there should be no child," Morgause answered at last.

"Do you truly believe that? Surely you wisewomen could have made sure any child she might conceive was not born!" He shook his head, temples beginning to pound with the sick headache that came from suppressing rage. "If death was a fit remedy for inappropriate conception, you should have hanged yourself on the nearest tree when you found yourself pregnant with me!

"You did not kill her because of my child, *Mother* . . . " all the bitterness Medraut had carried so long poured out at last, "but because of *yours*. I think you ordered Kea's death because you feared I might love her more than you!"

Morgause's hands fluttered outward in a little helpless gesture that snapped the last of his control.

"Well, you failed! I hate you, Queen-bitch, royal whore!" He flew at her and discovered that even without stirring she still had the power to stop him, shaking, where he stood.

"You are a prince! Show some control!"

"I am an abomination! I am what you have made me!"

"You will be free of me . . ." Morgause said tiredly. "I will not be returning to Dun Eidyn."

"Do you think that will make a difference, when every room holds your scent, and every stone the impress of your power. I am going south. Perhaps my *father* will teach me what it means to be a man. He could hardly do a worse job of it than you!"

The long hours in the saddle had given him the time to think it through. His mother had raised him to believe himself meant for a special destiny, and for two years now, he had thought himself true heir to Britannia. But in discovering her treachery, he had begun to question everything, and it had come to him that Artor's high seat was not hers to bestow. Neither would the inheritance come to him through Christian law. It was Artor himself he must persuade if he wanted his heritage.

"You will do nothing of the kind!" For the first time, Morgause looked alarmed. "You will stay in Alba and inherit the Votadini lands. Artor has all of your brothers. He does not need you."

"Do you still hate him, Mother?" Medraut asked maliciously. "Or has this conversion to holiness taken even that away?"

"Artor . . ." she said stiffly, "is no longer my concern."

"Nor am I, mother dear, nor am I . . ." Medraut's fury was fading, to be replaced by a cold detachment, as if the rage had burned all his humanity away. He liked the feeling—it took away the pain. "I am the age Artor was when he became king, no longer subject to a woman's rule. Will you lock me up to keep me from going where I choose?"

"If I have to—" Morgause said shortly.

Medraut laughed as she left him. But when he opened the door to follow, he found it guarded by two sturdy young women who looked as if they knew how to use the short spears gripped in their hands. In some things his mother's lessons still served him well. His first outraged response was suppressed so swiftly they scarcely noted it.

"Have you come to protect me? I am afraid my mother still considers me a child." He eyed them appreciatively and his smile became a complicit grin. They were young and, living among women, must be curious about beings of a gender they saw only at festivals. In another moment one of the girls began to smile back, and he knew that she, at least, was not seeing him as a child at all.

"Do not say that it serves me right, after all the trouble I gave you, to find an enemy in my son!" exclaimed Morgause, whirling to glare at Igierne, who sat still in her great carven chair. So still—even in the throes of her confusion, Morgause felt a pang. With each day Igierne seemed to grow more fragile, as if her substance was evaporating like the morning dew.

But her voice, when she replied, was strong. "Have I said

so? But if he is rebelling, surely you, of all mothers, ought to understand."

"That is not what has upset me. Medraut has grown as I shaped him, and now that I no longer desire to do so, I am afraid to loose him upon the world."

"You shaped him," observed the third woman, who had been sitting with Igierne when Morgause slammed through the door into the room. "But the wisefolk of my land teach that the Norns are three. You bear responsibility for what has been, maybe, but now your son is becoming a new person, and he must choose what shall be."

"What do you know of it, outlander?" Morgause spat back. Igierne lifted a hand in protest, and Morgause bit back her next words. She had grown unaccustomed to self-control.

Hæthwæge gazed back at her, unfazed, and Morgause glared. She had been raised to think of the Saxon kind as enemy, and found Hæthwæge's name and race alike disturbing, but Igierne had welcomed her, and in truth, the old woman who had helped to raise the child-king of Cantuware had knowledge they could use.

"I was not happy when the time came for me to give up Eormenric to the care of men—it still seems to me that seven is too young," Hæthwæge said then. "But it is true that a child needs the teaching of both male and female to grow. Let Medraut's father take him if he needs a stronger hand."

There was a short, charged silence.

"His father is the high king. . . ." Through clenched teeth Morgause got out the words.

"Ah—and he is your brother. . . ." Hæthwæge nodded. "I know that the Christians are not understanding about such things."

For a moment longer Morgause stared at her. Then she began, rather helplessly, to laugh. Weathered and bent like an old elder tree, Hæthwæge played the role of a simple village wisewoman very well, but Morgause could see past the mask. If the *wicce* had made light of the danger, it was on purpose, to comfort her.

She was trying to think of a polite rejoinder when there was a knock at the door. In the next moment it swung open and they saw Verica, one of the young priestesses who had been set to guard Medraut.

"He's gone!"

Morgause felt suddenly cold.

"Did he harm Cunovinda?" asked Igierne.

"Oh Vinda is just fine—unless you call a broken heart a wound," Verica said bitterly. "I left her guarding a locked door, and when I returned it was open and she was crying her eyes out because he had persuaded her to open it and then left her!"

It could have been worse, thought Morgause numbly. He could have taken the girl with him, and then killed or abandoned her. Who knew what Medraut might do?

"He is beyond your reach, daughter," Igierne said then, and Hæthwæge added, "He will make his own wyrd now. . . ."

"That is so, but this child's wyrd could shake a kingdom," said Igierne.

Morgause nodded. What that fate might be she dared not imagine, but she knew where he was going, and for the first time in her life, felt pity for Artor.

The high king of Britannia sat in his chair of state to receive the ambassadors. The basilica at Calleva would have been more impressive, or the one in Londinium, but the long chamber that had once been the pride of the commander of the fort at Isca had been restored when he rebuilt the town's defenses. The walls bore no frescoes, but they had been newly whitewashed, with a bright band of geometric designs painted along the top and bottom, and there were touches of gilding on the columns that ran down the nave. The cloaks of the chieftains and princes who had crowded inside, chequered and banded or bright with embroidery, made a vivid spectacle. Artor had been in Castra Legionis for a little over a month, long enough for everyone in the area who had a petition or a grievance to travel here.

But for this audience Artor had chosen to wear the full panoply of an emperor, and the length of time it had been since the previous occasion was marked by the difficulty they had in finding a jewel-sewn mantle in a shade that would match the deep green tunic, with its orphreys and apparels of gold woven brocade. That had been when they made peace with King Icel, said Betiver when Artor tried to remember. Then, thought the king as he tried to shift position without dislodging the stiff folds of the mantle, he had wanted to impress barbarians. Today his purpose was to appear as an heir of Rome's imperium before other heirs of Rome.

Artor felt Betiver stir nervously in his place behind the chair and turned his head to smile reassuringly.

"I should have been the one to welcome him," muttered the younger man. "But I didn't know what to say. Christ! It's been more than twenty years!"

Twenty years ago, Betiver had been an awestruck boy and Artor himself just learning to wield the power of a king, and now the child who had been left with him to seal an alliance was one of the supports of his kingdom.

"He is your father," Artor said aloud. "He will forgive. It is I who should earn his wrath for keeping you here—"

Then the great double doors at the end of the hall swung open, and men moved aside to clear an aisle as the embassy from Gallia marched in.

Johannes Rutilius seemed smaller than Artor remembered, worn by the years. For the men of Gallia, as for Britannia, those years had been filled by fighting. Rutilius walked with a limp now, and there was abundant silver in his hair. But he still stood erect, and the only change in his expression came when he realized who the warrior standing behind Artor must be.

But the formal Latin greetings did not falter, nor did Artor's welcome.

"Is your lord in good health?" he asked. "He must be ripe in years."

Rutilius sighed as he sank into the chair they brought for him. "He is old indeed, and not much time is left to him. Hence this embassy. When I came before, we offered you alliance. Now I come to ask for the help you swore to give. Riothamus is dying, my lord, but Chlodovechus of the Franks is in the flower of his age, seeking to extend the Frankish lands in the north, while Alaric II leads the Visigoths of Tolosa against us in the south.

"The only son of Riothamus, Daniel Dremrud, was killed some years ago, fighting in the German lands. My lord's grandsons intrigue against each other—" He cast a tired glance at a dark young man who stood glowering among the warriors who had escorted him into the hall.

"Budic, there, is one of them. Five years ago, he and his brother Maxentius attacked Civitas Aquilonia in the south of Armorica, to which they had a claim from their mother's father. Now Budic's brother has expelled him in turn. He hopes you will give him an army with which to take it back again."

"Then Riothamus is not asking my support for Budic as his heir?" asked Artor.

"We are Romans," Rutilius said simply: "And the Empire has always prospered when we sought heirs not of the body but of the spirit. Well, I know that it is so—does not my own son cleave to you before his own kin?"

He looked past Artor to Betiver, who flushed painfully, but he was smiling. He gestured towards Artor's mantle. "And I see that you, my lord, also hold to the spirit of Rome—so you will understand."

"What?" Artor said into the silence. "What does he wish of me?"

"You will make up your own mind whether to give aid to Budic in Aquilonia—but Riothamus judges neither of his grandsons of the stature to defend Gallia. The Emperor of the East is far away, and an Ostrogoth rules in Rome. The last strength of the West lies here, lord, in Britannia, where you have driven out the wild Irish and set the Saxon beneath your heel. What will your soldiers do now?"

There was a little stir among the watching warriors as Rutilius looked around.

"Bring them to Gallia, *princeps*, and Riothamus will make you his heir. Your fame is great in Armorica, and the grandsons of the men who followed Maximian will flock to your standard. Come to our aid, my lord Artor, and we will make you Emperor!"

The old dream reborn! Struggling to keep his face impassive, Artor sat back in his chair, the ghosts of Magnentius and Maximian, who had led the legions of Britannia to fight for the Empire, whispering in his ear. Constantine himself had been acclaimed in Eboracum before marching south to his destiny. Aegidius and his son Syagrius had tried to restore the Western Empire in Gallia, but without the resources of Britannia they could not endure. His foster-father Caius Turpilius had brought him up on these tales.

But with the power of Britannia and the blessing of Riothamus behind him, Artor might well succeed where no other man could. He had already succeeded in uniting Britannia, which neither Vitalinus nor Ambrosius nor Uthir had been able to do. Was it for this that he had been healed of his injury? He blinked, dazzled at the prospect. Oh, what a noble dream!

"My lord?" said a voice close by, and Artor forced his attention to the present once more.

"This is . . . an unexpected . . . offer," he managed to say. "It will require careful thought and discussion."

"Of course," answered Rutilius.

"You are my guest, and have scarcely tasted our hospitality," the king said in a more normal tone. "Let Betiver be my deputy, and do his duty to both of us in arranging for your lodging. Budic shall be our guest as well. Whatever the future may hold, I am still king in Britannia, and there are men waiting whose petitions I must hear."

Medraut ran his hand up the kitchen girl's leg beneath her skirts and pulled her back to the bed. "One more kiss—don't waste it. Once we reach the court you may never see me again."

"Let me go, you silly boy—I'll be late—" she protested, but she was laughing, and when he held her down and kissed her, she sighed and melted against him.

It was his turn to laugh, then, as a single smooth movement brought him off the bed and upright. He crossed to the basin he had made her bring to the room, and began to wash. It was little more than a cubbyhole, with a single pallet that would hold two people only if they were very friendly. But if Medraut had not had a knack for gaining what the Irish liked to call the "friendship of the thighs," he would not have been here.

He remembered, with momentary regret, the young priestess who had helped him to escape from the Isle of Maidens. Her kisses had been shy but sweet; it was too bad he had not had the time to take her maidenhead. To seduce one of the girls whose virginity his mother—the hypocrite—was guarding would have been a satisfactory first step to his revenge.

"You are mad," said the kitchen girl, who still lay on the bed with her skirts rucked up about her thighs. "The high king does not hand out places at his court to every nameless wanderer. Even the lord Goriat served for two seasons in the kitchen."

"Oh, I have a name," answered Medraut, "though I have not shared it with you." In truth, he had already forgotten hers. "But Goriat will no doubt remember you. Bring me to him, and you will have done all I require."

"Oh, you *are* a proud one!" she exclaimed, lifting her chin with a mocking sniff. "I will bring you to my lord, and see how far you fly when he throws you out the door!"

Ignoring her, Medraut went to his pack and pulled out the garments he had carried all the way from Dun Eidyn. At the flare of crimson silk, the girl fell silent, her eyes widening as he pulled on breeches of finely woven brown wool and shoes of tooled calfskin whose laces criss-crossed up his calves. The silk unrolled into a tunic, ornamented at shoulders and hem with bands embroidered with silver thread. From the folds of his chequered mantle he pulled a silver torc, and twisting, slid it around his neck, pulled a comb through his dark auburn hair and picked up the mantle.

"Who *are* you?" breathed the girl.

"Take me to Goriat, and you may learn—" Medraut gave her a sardonic smile. "If you remember what I told you to say. . . ."

During the time it took for her to lead him from the cubbyhole in the old barracks through the narrow lanes of the fortress to the wide porch before the audience hall he refused to say another word.

He had learned that Gualchmai was newly wedded, and away on his wife's lands in the south, and Aggarban still on sick leave. That did not matter. It was Goriat who would be most likely to recognize him, and who must stand, however reluctantly, his ally. He had no difficulty recognizing him, standing with Gwyhir in the midst of laughing warriors, for his brothers overtopped most of the other men by a head.

Only the court and its servants could enter. He had to depend on the girl to make her way through the men to Goriat. He saw his brother turn, frowning. Medraut grinned. He had told the girl to say a message had come for "Dandelion," Goriat's baby-name, but he gave it in the dialect of the north. In another moment both of his brothers were pushing through the crowd.

"It's the brat!" exclaimed Goriat, staring at Medraut. Then he looked anxiously around him. "Where's Mother?"

"With the holy bitches at the Lake, rump aimed at the moon and nose in the dust, muttering sorceries. . . ."

"Oh . . . my . . . mother's baby boy has fled the nest indeed!" breathed Gwyhir. "I thought that you at least would stay with her in Dun Eidyn!"

"I thought she would have married you off to a Pictish princess by now," said Goriat. "That's what she tried to do to me!"

He blinked at the venom in Medraut's answering glare, but it was quickly quenched. There was no way, he thought, that Goriat could know about Kea.

"I do hope that Gualchmai was not expecting to stand on the Votadini coronation stone—" he said aloud. "Cunobelinus rules there now, and even for Leudonus' son I do not think he will give it up again."

"And Mother did not fight it? She simply walked away?" repeated Gwyhir in amazement. "Has she gone mad?"

Medraut shrugged. When, he wondered, had Morgause ever been sane?

"I have come south to seek my fortune with the rest of you," he said then. "They say that our mother's brother is throned on high in yonder hall. Will not one of you escort me there and make the introductions?"

*　*　*

The messenger from Dun Breatann had been speaking for some time. Artor focused his attention with an effort as a change in the man's voice heralded a conclusion. "And so, it is the request of my master Ridarchus that the high king journey to confer with him on this matter—"

What matter? Artor had been thinking of Gallia and had scarcely heard. The Irish—that was it—the king of the Dal Riadans had offered alliance. He cleared his throat and straightened.

"I will consider Ridarchus' request, but it is my judgment that the men of Eriu will lie quiet at least until next spring. I will come, but I must consider the needs of the rest of Britannia before I decide on when."

That was a tactful answer that would not bind him, but it was true. Even if he decided to accept Riothamus' offer, he must spend some time settling things here before he could leave. Perhaps Betiver could lead a token force to Gallia. . . .

The man from Dun Breatann bowed and backed away. The crowd stirred, and he saw the fair heads of Goriat and Gwyhir moving above the others like swans on a stream.

"My lord uncle!" called Gwyhir. "We have brought a new recruit to your service!"

Another man was with them—no, a boy just beginning his growth spurt, with dark red hair. Artor caught the gleam of a silver torc, but the features were a blur. His heart pounded suddenly, as if he had come upon an enemy unaware.

"The last of my mother's sons has come south to join us," added Goriat heartily. "Here is Medraut, lord king. Will you welcome him?"

Artor stared down at the boy's bent head. He had recognized him already, without yet understanding. But how had the time passed so quickly? This boy was almost grown! Medraut did not resemble his brothers, though there was the promise of height in those long bones. But as he began to get up, the king suppressed an instinctive recoil, for in that fine-boned face he saw Morgause. He wondered if his sister had told her son the truth about his parentage.

"Is it your wish to serve me, boy?" His voice sounded harsh in his own ears.

"You shall be as a father to me . . ." answered Medraut, and smiled.

A CIRCLE OF KINGS

A·D· 503

THE PLAIN STRETCHED AWAY TO A GREY LINE OF HILLS, A NEW layer of green grass poking through last year's trampled straw. Medraut's mare jerked at the rein, reaching for a bite, and he hauled up her head. Since joining Artor's court the previous autumn he had gotten a lot more practice in riding. Even in winter the high king moved often, and his household went with him. Medraut found these southern lands fair and fat, with their thick woods and fertile fields, but to one accustomed to the harsh vistas of the north, their very luxuriance felt confining.

From Castra Legionis they had travelled south to Dumnonia, and then to Camalot for the Midwinter holy days. He wished they could have stayed there, for Artor's queen had been kind to him. Guendivar's golden beauty reminded him of his lost Kea. But perhaps it was just as well they did not stay long, he thought then. She might not have been so friendly if someone had told her he was Artor's son.

If so, he had only himself to blame, he thought ruefully. Or perhaps his brothers—when they persisted in treating him as if he were still a child there had been a stupid argument, and he had retorted that of them all, only he and Gualchmai could truly say who their fathers had been. They had only agreed to keep silent on the matter after tempers had cooled, but someone must have overheard. He could tell by the way people looked at him, afterward.

He would not make that mistake again, he told himself, shifting in the saddle. And yet perhaps it was just as well, if Artor was going to acknowledge him, that the news did not come as a complete surprise.

They had finished the winter in Londinium, and now they were on their way north once more. But the straightest way to Alba would have been to follow the old Roman road to Lindum, through the Anglian lands. Instead, the royal party had turned west through Calleva to Sorviodunum before taking the track that led north to this plain, the largest expanse of open land in Britannia.

Medraut shivered. It was cold here, with nothing to break the wind. Even at high summer, he suspected, that wind would blow. Now, a week after the Feast of the Resurrection, the wind probed the weave of his cloak with chill fingers and whispered like a restless soul.

Ahead he could see the first of the barrows that marched across the plain. Perhaps that was why the thought had come to him. He grimaced. His mother would have welcomed the ghosts, avid and smiling. His ... father ... riding near the head of the line, sat his big black horse easily, his watchful gaze revealing no emotion at all.

Medraut squeezed the red mare's sides and moved forward. There was plenty of room to go abreast, and the warrior who had been riding nearest reined aside to let him bring his mare up next to the king. Artor's grey gaze flickered towards him and away.

Do I make you uneasy, my father-uncle? The king had made him welcome with the greatest courtesy, but there was always a tension between them. Was it guilt that made Artor so wary, wondered Medraut, or had his mother warped him into something that no one could love?

"This is not the way to Glevum—" he said aloud.

"Not the most direct, it is true," Artor replied.

"Then why have we come here? No doubt it is very interesting, but is your kingdom so peaceful that you can waste time sightseeing? I thought you were eager to see the land settled so that you could go to Gallia—"

"When Maximian set out to claim the Imperium, the wild tribes of the north attacked like wolves when the shepherd has left the fold. Until I am satisfied regarding our defenses, I will not leave these shores. Betiver and the men he has taken yonder will bolster Riothamus until I come."

"Betiver is the old man's sister-son—" Medraut observed with a sidelong smile. "Are you not afraid that Riothamus will make him his heir?"

"It would be very natural," Artor said softly, his gaze still on the land ahead. "If that should come to pass I would rejoice for Betiver and swear alliance gladly, though I would miss his presence at my side."

Medraut's heart raced in his breast. *He means to make me his heir! I am sure of it, or why would he be talking to me this way?*

"There—" said Artor as they reached the top of the rise. "That is why we have come here."

Medraut straightened, shading his eyes with his hand. To their right, the line of barrows stretched away across the plain. The nearest was larger than the others, its sides still rough beneath the furring of grass, as if it had not yet had time to settle completely into the land.

"These are the graves of ancient kings, gone back to the earth of the land they loved."

Medraut shivered as he heard the echo of his thoughts in Artor's words.

"The mound at the end holds the bones of the British princes whom Hengest killed by treachery on the Night of the Long Knives. My uncle Ambrosius is buried there, and Uthir, my father, as well."

My grandfather . . . thought Medraut. This was a heritage his mother did not share, and he looked at the mound curiously, trying to remember what he had heard about those long ago days when the Saxons had overrun the land in blood and fire.

"Well, you have avenged them," he said then. "The Saxon wolf is tamed."

"For now," Artor agreed. "While we stay strong. But in

Gallia, the Franks and Burgunds and Visigoths that were settled on the land to defend it rule the Romans now. They may
pretend to adopt our ways, but even Oesc—" He broke off,
shaking his head. Then he gestured towards the mounds. "It
will take time to make us all one people. When the bones of
Saxon and Briton are mingled together with the dust of this
land perhaps we may trust them. But it will take time."

Medraut looked at him skeptically. Old men, he had heard,
tended to live in the past. The high king looked strong, but
there was silver in his beard. Was he getting old?

The wind blew more strongly. From overhead he heard the
harsh cry of a raven and looked upward. The bird circled the
riders once and then flapped away to the westward. Medraut,
turning to track its flight, stilled, staring at the circle of stones
that seemed to have risen out of the ground. He had seen
Roman buildings that were larger, but never such mighty
pieces of stone. Standing proud as kings come to council, their
stark simplicity chilled his soul.

Something in his silence must have alerted the king, for
Artor followed his gaze and smiled.

"It is the Giant's Dance. Merlin brought me here when I
was a boy."

Medraut twitched involuntarily at the sound of that name.
The Druid had arrived at Castra Legionis not long after he
himself had come there. There was no reason to think it had
anything to do with him. Men said that Merlin had always
come and gone at his own will—not even the high king could
command him. But there was something in the dark stare
beneath those bushy brows that made Medraut feel naked.
He had been surprised at the depth of his own relief when
the old man went away once more.

"Why?" he asked baldly.

Artor looked at him, one eyebrow lifting. "Come and see—"
With a word to Cai, he reined his horse towards the stone circle, and after a moment's astonished hesitation, Medraut followed.

As he neared the circle, he looked over his shoulder. The
rest of the column was continuing its march across the plain.
The boy looked around him nervously. Had the king decided

he posed too great a danger and found this opportunity to get rid of him? Reason told him it was unlikely. Artor could have gotten away with such a deed far more easily in Londinium than this empty land where everyone would know.

"Don't be afraid," said Artor, interpreting his hesitation correctly even if, one hoped, he did not divine its cause. He pulled up before a stone that stood in front of the others like a sentinel, slid off of his mount and motioned to Medraut to do the same. "At this time of day and at this season, the circle is not dangerous."

Medraut started forward. As he passed through the outer circle of uprights he flinched. A buzz, more felt than heard, vibrated through his bones.

"Don't you feel it?" he asked as Artor turned inquiringly. "This place is warded."

"Not precisely—Merlin says that a current of power flows between the stones. I have learned to sense such things, but when I was your age I could not feel it. Is this a natural talent, Medraut, or *her* teaching?"

The boy felt himself flushing. No need to ask whom he meant. What had his mother done to Artor to make *him* fear her? He took another step towards the middle trilithon. Everything beyond the circle appeared to waver, as if he were looking at it through glass.

"Wait—" Artor set his hand on Medraut's shoulder. He twitched, but the touch steadied him, and he did not pull away. Together, they moved between the huge capped uprights of the inner circle into the level space within. As they neared the altar stone Medraut sensed a subliminal hum, as if he were standing next to a hive of bees.

Artor's gaze had gone inward. "Power flows beneath the soil as water flows through riverbeds, from circle to circle, and from stone to stone. Here, two great currents cross. It is a place of mighty magic."

"Have you brought my brothers here?" Medraut asked softly after a time, still anchored by the king's hand.

Artor shook his head.

"You know, don't you ..." Medraut said then, "about me. ..."

For the first time, he allowed himself to stare at the man who had fathered him. The high king, if not quite so tall as Medraut's older brothers, was still bigger than most men, his torso heavy with muscle. His features were too rugged for beauty, weathered by years of responsibility into a mask of power. But there were laughter lines around the grey eyes that watched him from beneath level brows. Except, perhaps, in those eyes, he could see nothing of himself in this man at all.

The king let go of his shoulder, looking away. "She did not tell me you existed until you were ten years old."

"Why didn't you take me away from her?"

"I had no proof . . ." Artor whispered.

At ten, Medraut had still believed that his mother was good, and that he himself would grow up to be a hero one day. If the king had taken him then, his son might have been able to love him.

"You were newly married and expected to get a legitimate child," he said flatly. "But you have none. Will you make me your heir?"

"You have a son's claim on me, Medraut. But I am more a Roman than a Briton when it comes to the Imperium. They did not make me king because I was my father's son, or not wholly, but because of the Sword."

Artor's hand settled over the pommel of the blade at his side, and Medraut shivered as a new note pierced the circle's hum, so high and clear that it hurt to hear. He knew about the Sword, of course, but it was always the Cauldron that his mother had coveted. This was man's magic, and this too, he thought with a tremor of excitement, was his heritage.

The sound faded as the high king's hand moved once more to his side, and he sighed. "When the time comes, if there is a man fit to hold it, he will become the Defender of Britannia. I will do what I can for you, but I can make no promises."

Medraut frowned. *If you had raised me, Father, I might believe that. But in the North we know that bloodright binds the king to his land. Britannia belongs to me. . . .* But he did not voice those thoughts aloud.

* * *

The road from Mamucium to Bremetennacum led through low hills. The king and his escort had spent the night in the abandoned fort above the river. The timber barracks buildings had long ago collapsed, but the gatehouse and parts of the praetorium, where once the commander of the garrison had ruled, still provided some shelter. But it was a cheerless camp, for the town outside the walls had fallen into ruin a generation before.

It was fear that had killed the town, thought Artor, not the Saxons, for there was no sign of burning. The people who had once inhabited those mute, overgrown heaps of rubble had simply moved away. *But they will return . . .* he told himself. *The site on the river is a good one. From these ruins some day a mighty city will rise.*

Something moved in the tangle of hazels that flanked the road. By the time he identified the whistle of arrows Artor was already turning, flattening himself against the stallion's neck as he grabbed for his shield. A horse squealed, rearing. Behind him a man slid from his mount, a black-feathered arrow jutting from his chest. Artor straightened, peering back down the line from the shelter of his shield. He sighed with unexpected relief as he saw that Medraut, who had been riding with Goriat, had his shield up as well.

An arrow thunked into his own, and he realized that the enemy were concentrating their fire on the forward part of the line. Masterless men who lived by banditry, he thought. This time they had chosen the wrong prey.

"Vanguard, dismount!" he cried. "Goriat, take your riders and hit them from the rear!"

He slid from the saddle. A swat sent Raven trotting down the road. Afoot, Artor and his men were smaller targets. Though he had no recollection of drawing it, his sword was in his hand. It flared in the sunlight as he ran towards the trees.

Branches thrashed, scratching his shield. Artor crashed through them, glimpsed a man's shape and thrust. The blade bit and someone yelled. The king jerked the sword free and pushed onward. From ahead came more yelling. He cut down two more enemies before he reached the clearing where the horsemen had caught the fleeing men.

Several bodies lay crumpled on the grass. The fifteen or so outlaws who remained glared at the horsemen whose circle held them, lances pointing at their breasts. The king straightened, shield still up, waiting for his pulse to slow. It was more than a year since he had drawn his sword in anger; the fading rush of battle fury warred with the ache of stressed muscles and the smart where a branch had whipped across his brow.

That felt too good— he thought wryly, *like the first beaker of beer at the end of a long, hot day.* Automatically, he was making a headcount of friend and foe. He noted Medraut's auburn head and once more, tension he had not been aware of suddenly eased. Why? There were others—Betiver or Gualchmai—whom he loved better than he did this sullen boy, but he had never sagged with relief after a fight to find them still alive.

Medraut's face was pale with excitement, his eyes burning like coals. A bloodstained scarf was tied around his arm. Artor swallowed as he saw it. He would have to get the boy some armor. The others were his friends, but this boy was his future. *I have a hostage to fortune now.*

He shook himself and strode forward. "Cai, get rope to bind them."

The prisoners were a sorry lot, stinking and unshaven, clad in tattered wool and badly cured leather. One man was missing an ear. But the weapons they had thrown down looked well-used.

"We're poor men, lord—" whined one of the prisoners, "refugees from the Saxon wars."

"Indeed? It seems to me that you speak like a man of Glevum—"

"My father was from Camulodunum," the complainer said quickly. "He was a sandalmaker there. But the towns are dying, and where shall I practice the trade he taught me now? Surely you'll not be too harsh with folk who are only trying to survive!"

"Work then!" Artor said harshly. "Britannia is full of abandoned farms. Learn to get food by the sweat of your own brows, rather than taking it from better men! You complain that there are no towns!" He shook his head in disgust. "When you make the roads unsafe for honest travelers, how in the Lady's name do you expect towns to survive?"

"Shall we hang them here, lord?" called one of the horsemen, and the robber's face showed his fear.

Artor shook his head. "There is still a magistrate at Bremetennacum. These wretches shall be judged by the people on whom they have preyed."

There was blood on his blade, but it seemed to him he could feel a hum of satisfaction from the sword. Carefully he wiped it and slid it into the sheath once more. When he looked up, he met Medraut's considering gaze.

He says he will not make me his heir, thought Medraut, watching the high king as he took his place on the bench the monks had set out for him, *but why has he brought me along on this journey if not to show me what it is to be a king?*

Gaining Artor's throne was not going to be easy. The gash where the arrow had nicked his arm throbbed dully and he adjusted the sling to support it, remembering the first shock of pain, and the next even more disturbing awareness that the arrow had come from behind. He had said nothing to Artor, for he could prove nothing. But the psychic defenses honed by years with Morgause had snapped back into place like a king's houseguard. It was only when he felt that familiar wary tension return that he realized that traveling with his father, he had begun to let them down.

The fort at Bremetennacum had fallen into ruin, but the townsfolk here had managed to maintain their ditch and palisade. Perhaps the reason was the rich bottomlands of the valley and the river with its easy access to the sea. The land was good here, and so was the trade, but that only made the place a more attractive target for raids. The magistrates who had been seated on their own benches beside him gazed sourly around them, torn between gratitude to the king for capturing the robbers and resentment of the pace at which they were required to deal with them.

They had sentenced the leaders to hang, but the remainder

they enslaved, arguing that it was justice that those who had stolen the fruit of others' labors should be denied the use of their own. As the last of the prisoners was marched off to death or servitude, the townsmen straightened, anticipating the feast that had been prepared to honor their visitor.

But Artor was not yet done with them.

"We've cleared out one nest of vermin, and you and your goods will have safe passage to Mamucium and Deva—for a time. But what happens when some other ruffian decides to settle in? I cannot be everywhere, and who will protect you then?"

"We are merchants and farmers, lord, not fighting men—" one of the magistrates said sullenly. He gestured in the direction in which the prisoners had gone. "If we were, do you think we would have suffered that lot for so long?"

"If you cannot defend yourselves, then I will have to appoint you a protector . . ." the king said slowly. "Is that what you desire?"

"Oh, my lord—" Another man looked up eagerly. "Indeed it is! He and his men can stay at the old fort, and—"

Artor's features creased in a sardonic smile, as if he had heard this before. "And who will rebuild it? And what will they eat? An ill-fed man cannot swing a sword—"

"But you— We supposed—" The magistrates wilted beneath his glare.

"I will give you Paulinus Clutorix, a veteran of the Saxon wars, and three experienced men."

"But that's not enough—"

"Very true," Artor continued briskly. "He will take on more, enough to mount a regular patrol, and he will drill every man of fighting age in this valley in the use of arms so that when the time comes to go after a band of outlaws, or you see yon river bobbing with Irish coracles, you'll have a force sufficient to deal with them."

The town fathers were frowning. Their reluctance seemed strange to Medraut, who had grown up among a warrior people who had never been forbidden by the Romans to bear arms. But he could see that some of the younger men were grinning. He had seen his father fight the day before. Now, he was seeing how Artor ruled.

"And there will be a levy, in goods or coin, upon each household for their keep." The townsmen began to protest while Artor's warriors tried to hide their grins. The king held up one hand. "Did you assume I would send gold? How do you think I feed my men if not by taking tithes and levying taxes? At least this way you will know where your tax money goes. And the burden must be shared by everyone—" He gazed sternly around him. "Even the monks who own these rich fields...."

Now it was the churchmen who were protesting. The defending force would have their prayers, of course, but their produce belonged to God. In Artor's face there was no yielding. Medraut suppressed an anticipatory grin.

"Good father, if prayer had protected you from outlaw spears or Irish swords I might agree," said the king. "But I have seen too many burnt monasteries. Pay your share, holy brethren, if you expect my men to come to your call!" He sat back, eyes glinting, a grim smile twitching the brown beard.

Morgause had always said that Artor let the priests rule him, but Medraut saw now that it was not so. He sat hunched on his bench, resting his chin on his fist as he watched. In how many other ways had she been wrong? The priests would call his birth ungodly, but he was *glad* now to be Artor's son. And if he worked hard, he thought, perhaps the wary courtesy with which the high king treated him would change to true affection, and Medraut could prove himself a worthy heir....

"It looks ... defensible ..." said Gwyhir, whose turn it was to ride beside the king.

Artor laughed. The firth of the Clutha lay before them, its waters a shifting sheet of silver beneath the high clouds. Low hills ran along the peninsula behind it, featureless as if carved from shadow. The great rock of Altaclutha rose from those opalescent waters like an island, its sheer sides carved by the gods into a fortress that needed little help from man to be secure. From this distance, he could scarcely distinguish the stone walls and slate roofs from the native stone, and the causeway that connected it to the land was hidden from view.

"Dun Breatann is the fortress of the Britons indeed. Since my father's time the Rock has guarded the west of Alba. But Ridarchus is old now, and I do not know his heir."

"It is Morcant Bulc, is it not?" Gwyhir answered him. "Ridarchus' grandson. They came once to Dun Eidyn when I was a child."

Artor nodded. He did not want to think about inheritance, but he supposed it was his duty. Unbidden, the face of Medraut came to mind. He had hoped to learn more of the boy on this long journey up from the south, and to some extent he had done so. But Medraut's smooth surface repelled intimacy. How he could have come from the same nest as his brothers was cause for amazement. Gualchmai could not conceal a thought if he tried. Aggarban's sullen silences were easily read, and the eyes of Gwyhir and Goriat were deep pools into which one had only to gaze to see their souls.

Medraut was clearly doing his best to please, thought the king. He was observant, and did not make the same mistake twice, but he reminded the king of a man struggling to learn a new language, learning by rote the turns of phrase for which he had no natural ear. It was not because he had been brought up in Alba—his brothers had been accepted by Artor's household immediately. But their actions, even their mistakes, came from the heart. One sensed that Medraut's were the result of calculation.

In the next moment Artor shook his head, blaming his distrust on his own fears. Most likely the boy was simply shy.

The high king glanced back along the line. Men who had been slumped in the saddle reined in straying mounts and straightened to military alertness when they felt his eye upon them. Artor turned back, gesturing to Gwyhir to blow his horn. The sound echoed across the pewter waters, and in a few moments he heard an answer from the dun, faint and sweet with distance, like an echo of faerie horns.

The night after their arrival a storm rolled in from the sea, dense clouds wrapping close about the Rock, blanketing the

ever-changing tides. For five days they huddled beneath the
slate roofs of the fortress, the only thing solid in a dissolving
world. But the ale-vats of Dun Breatann were deep, and if it
was wet outside, the drink flowed just as freely within.

"I gather that your journey here was not altogether peaceful—" said Ridarchus, indicating the bits of bandage that still
adorned some of Artor's men.

Unlike his brother-in-law, Merlin, who still towered like a
tree, Ridarchus had shrunk with the years, flesh and bone
fined down to a twisted, sinewy frame. Only his nose still
jutted fiercely. Sitting there with his black mantle and glinting
dark eyes he reminded Artor of a raven. And like the bird,
Ridarchus had grown wise with years.

"It's true, and makes your hospitality all the more welcome.
But you will find the roads to the south safer, for awhile."

"You should have found them safe already, once you entered my lands," rasped Ridarchus. "I must thank you for
ridding me of young Cuil and his band. But his death has
won you few friends here, I warn you. He was popular with
the common folk, with whom he used to share his booty."

"Do they not understand that without safe roads there will
be no trade, and no long-term prosperity?"

"In their children's time, perhaps," said the prince, "but
Cuil gave them gifts they could hold in their hands."

"I suppose so, and I am sorry he was killed in the fighting,"
said Artor, "for he was the brother of a man who captained
the queen's guard when we campaigned in Demetia, and after
I had drawn his teeth I would have spared him." He blinked
as a change in the wind outside rippled through the hangings
that were supposed to keep out draughts and sent smoke
billowing sideways from the central fire.

"Maybe now news will reach us as well," said Ridarchus.
"We hear little of what is happening in the world outside this
isle."

Artor shook his head. "The Empire of the West is beseiged
on every side. Theoderic rules in Italia, and has just married
his daughter Amalafrida to Thraseric of the Vandals in the
north of Africa. In Gallia, Chlodovechus is expanding his bor-

ders in all directions. Three years ago he captured Burdigala. They say that the Romans in the Gothic lands fought for Alaric, their Gothic ruler, but the Franks were still too strong for them. Alaric made peace and paid Chlodovechus tribute last year."

"Will the Visigoths become a subject kingdom then?"

Artor shrugged. "They have a foothold in Iberia already— they have moved so many times, perhaps they will all pass over the Pyrenaei montes and abandon the south of Gallia to the Franks entirely."

The men who sat around the fire were singing, first the warriors from the dun, and then, as they caught the chorus, Artor's men as well. The king did not see Medraut among them and wondered where he had gone.

"I perceive that this matters to you," Ridarchus said after a moment had passed. "But we have our own troubles here in Britannia. Why do you care what happens across the sea?"

"No doubt Cassivellaunus might have said the same, before Caesar came," Artor observed dryly. "The Franks have proved themselves a warlike people. If they are not controlled now, your son's sons may see them at your gates. And there are men of our blood in Gallia who will certainly be overrun."

"I have heard a rumor that you mean to cross the sea yourself." Ridarchus cocked his head, bright eyes fixing the king.

"Riothamus has appealed to me. But before I go I must make Britannia secure."

"Hence this journey—" Ridarchus said slowly.

The high king nodded. "Until the Saxons came, the wild tribes of the North were always the greatest danger, and after them, the men of Eriu. When I have done what I can for you, I will move on to Dun Eidyn and seek a treaty with the Pictish king."

Ridarchus signaled to one of the serving girls to bring them more ale. He drank, then set his beaker down with an appreciative sigh.

"You can make a treaty for me, too, if you will—" he said then. "You know that for many years there have been men of Eriu on the peninsula of Cendtire, the old Epidii lands. Far from increasing the danger from their kinfolk across the water, I think they have protected us. They have been good neighbors, and we have fought side by side when the Picts got too strong. But perhaps too many of them have left Dal Riada, for in Eriu, Feragussos their king can no longer hold against the Ui Niall.

"Do you see those two men in the saffron tunics, there by the door?" He paused to drink once more and Artor followed the direction of his gaze. "They arrived a little before you did. They are men of Cendtire, ambassadors. Feragussos wishes to move himself and his court and the rest of his clan here from Dal Riada, and offers friendship. I could tolerate their presence unofficially, but I would not enter into such an alliance without your good will."

Particularly, thought Artor, *when I am sitting in your hall.* But he smiled. "I agree. I shall prepare a letter of invitation to Feragussos and welcome him as an ally."

Medraut moved away from the shelter of the inner wall, leaning against the wind. For the moment it had ceased to rain, but there was still enough moisture in the air to sting. He picked his way across the uneven rock to the breast-high wall that edged the clifftop and clung to it, gulping deep breaths of the brisk wind.

To the south and west stretched the silver dimpled waters of the Clutha. Beneath banks of low cloud he could just make out the darker masses of the far shore. He looked up as a gull screamed overhead, flung across the sky by the wind.

Free— he thought, *what would it feel like to be that free?* Even through the thick folds of his woolen mantle he was beginning to feel the chill, but after the odorous warmth of the hall it was welcome. He turned, his gaze moving from the watchtower on the highest point of the Rock to the great hall set into the niche halfway down one side.

He wondered why he felt so constricted—he could find no fault with Ridarchus' hospitality . . . and then, as the gull called again, he remembered the seabirds wheeling above the Bodotria, and realized it was the scent of northern fires, and the sound of northern voices, that had disturbed him. They reminded him of Dun Eidyn.

I can't go back there, he thought, and still less did he desire to revisit Pictland, where he would remember Kea every time he turned around. But where could he run to? Certainly not to his mother. He had proved that he could manage on his own, but then he had been traveling with a goal, a place at the court of the high king. It was no part of his life-plan to become a nameless wanderer upon the roads. He wondered if Gualchmai and his new wife would take him in.

The sky was darkening. He felt one cold drop strike his hand and then a spattering of others as the heavens began to open once more. He sucked in a last breath of the cold, salt-tanged air and started back towards the inner wall. The squall was coming quickly now; he pulled his mantle over his head and hunched against the rain.

After the wall, one gained the next level by a steep flight of steps cut into the rock. Fighting the buffeting of the wind, Medraut had nearly gained the top when he sensed something dark rise up before him, recoiled, and slipped on the rain-slick stone. He flailed wildly, but there was nothing to hold onto. His falling body hit one outcrop and then another, and slid to the base of the wall.

When he came to himself, it was full dark. He hurt all over, and he was *cold.* Head throbbing, he tried to remember what had happened. If someone had pushed him, why had they not taken advantage of his unconsciousness to toss him into the sea? And if not, why was he still lying here? But if no one had seen him fall, surely someone should be wondering where he had gone. . . .

At least he could feel all his limbs. Very carefully, he tried to move. Everything ached, but it was only in his right leg that he felt real pain. Still, it was only going to get colder. He had to get up somehow.

Medraut had made it to the steps when he heard voices from above. Torches flared wildly as the wind caught them. Someone was calling his name.

"Look, there at the foot of the stair," someone cried.

"Here—" He let his dark mantle fall back so that the paler tunic could be seen. "I'm here. . . ."

He tensed as someone hurried towards him, torch held too

high for features to be seen. Then the man was kneeling, and Medraut looked up into the anxious eyes of Artor the king.

The storm had passed, but the high king of Britannia remained at Dun Breatann. The boy, Medraut, had broken his leg, and was not yet fit to ride. That Artor should stay for the sake of a nephew was a matter of wonder, but presently men began to speak of a greater wonder, that the nephew was also a son. Artor knew they said it, though he did not know from whom the rumor first had come. It was inevitable, he thought, that the truth would eventually be known. That did not disturb him so much as the whisper he had heard as he lifted his son in his arms.

"*Still living? A pity—if the bastard broke his neck it would be better for the king and for us all!*"

Artor had not recognized the voice, and the situation could only be made worse by questioning, but in the dark hours of the night he lay wakeful, remembering the moment of thought, instantly suppressed, in which he had hoped it might be true.

He was still there a week later, when horns proclaimed the arrival of another party and the Saxon lords rode in. When Artor had spoken with them he went to the terrace where Medraut, his leg splinted and bound, sat looking out at the sea.

"Who has come?" asked the boy, looking up at him.

Artor continued to gaze at the bright glitter of sun on water. "The brother of Cynric, who rules the south Saxons now," he said without turning. "I had sent to them before we left Londinium, requesting his son as hostage, to guarantee the peace while I am in Gallia."

"And he has refused?"

Artor shook his head, turning to face his son. "They have brought me the boy. Ceawlin is his name."

"Then why are you troubled? And why are you telling this to me?" Medraut swung his splinted leg down from the bench and sat up, the sunlight sparking on his hair in glints of fire.

Artor stared at him, striving to see past the coloring and

the fine bones that reminded him so painfully of Morgause. *Who are you really, boy? What is going on behind those eyes?*

"He desires me to send a man of my own kindred in exchange—'*to increase understanding between our peoples. . . .*' "

"And Goriat doesn't want to go, so you are thinking of sending me?" Medraut asked mockingly, and Artor felt his face grow red.

"Were you pushed down those stairs?" He held the boy's gaze and saw a glimmer of some emotion, swiftly shut away.

Artor had been king since he was the same age as this boy and he thought he knew how to judge men, but Medraut's personality offered no point of attachment on which to build a relationship.

Is that really true? he asked himself suddenly. *Or is it that you have been afraid to try?* He had kept the boy with him for almost a year, but how much time together had they really had?

After a moment, Medraut looked down.

"It was dark and raining . . . I thought there was someone, but I could not really see. I will tell you this, though. The arrow that wounded me in the south came from behind."

"You did not tell me!" Artor took a step forward, frowning, but Medraut's eyes were limpid as the sea.

"I had no proof, my lord, nor do I now. . . ."

Artor stood over him, fists clenching. *What are you hiding?* he thought, and then, *What am I?* He felt a vast weariness as his anger drained away.

"I will send you to the Saxons. Here, I cannot guarantee your safety, but Cynric will guard you like a she-wolf her last cub." *Against his own people, and mine,* his thought went on, *and perhaps against me. . . .*

"If you wish it, I will obey," answered Medraut, looking away.

Artor eyed at him narrowly, hearing in the boy's voice something almost like satisfaction, and wondered why.

III

IN THE PLACE OF STONES

A·D· 503

To travel across the neck of Alba in high summer, neither pursued nor pursuing, was pure pleasure. The Roman
forts that had once defended the Antonine Wall were now no
more than dimpled mounds, but the road that connected
them was still passable. To the north rose the outriders of the
highlands, blue with distance, the nearer slopes cloaked like
an emperor in heather. Alba was all purple and gold beneath
a pale northern sky, and the air had the same sweet tang as
the peat-brown waters that rippled down from the hills.

Artor breathed deeply and sat straighter, as cares he had
not known he carried fell away. Even the weather held fair,
as if to welcome him.

"It won't last," said Goriat. "A week, or two, and we'll see
fog and rain so thick you'd think it was winter in the southern
lands."

"All the more reason to enjoy it now!" Artor grinned back
at him, and Raven, sensing his rider's mood, pranced and
pulled at the rein. "By the time the weather changes, we'll be
safe at Fodreu."

Cai, who was riding on his other side, made a sound halfway between a grunt and a growl. "If we can trust them—I still say you're a fool to put yourself in their power!"

Goriat opened his eyes at the language, but Artor only smiled. There were times when Cai forgot the king was not still the little foster-brother who had followed him about when they were young. But the blood Cai had shed in his service since then, thought Artor, entitled him to a few blunt words. He was only four years older than the king, but he looked ten, the dark hair grizzled, and his face weathered and lined.

"Maybe so," Artor answered mildly, "but if they can't be trusted, better to find out now than have them break the border while I'm in Gallia!"

"Hmph!" Cai replied. "Or else you just enjoy the risk. I remember how it was when we were boys . . ."

Goriat kicked his horse in the ribs and drew level, brows quirked enquiringly.

"Whenever things got too quiet, Artor would find some fool thing to do. . . ." Cai exchanged rueful smiles with the king.

"Was I that bad?" asked Artor.

"Remember the miller's donkey?"

Artor's grin grew broader.

"What did he do?" asked Goriat in an awed voice.

"Tied the donkey to a threshing flail—"

"It could have worked," protested the king. "We use oxen to grind the corn, after all."

"What happened?" Goriat persisted, obviously delighted to be let in on this secret history.

"The donkey ate the grain and both Artor and I got a beating. They said I should have stopped him, but I knew even then the futility of trying to change Artor's mind when he gets that look in his eye," Cai answered resignedly.

"I learned something, though . . ." Artor continued after a moment had passed. "Beasts, or men, must be led in the direction their nature compels them. It is my judgment that the Picts are ready for peace. I would hate to think that I have grown so accustomed to fighting that I crave it as a drunkard his wine! Still, just in case, Cai has the right of it: there is one whom I have no right to lead into danger—" He glanced back down the line, seeking the gleam of Ceawlin's ruddy hair.

"Goriat, go back down the line and bring Cynric's cub up here to ride with me."

"And that's another risk . . ." mumured Cai as the younger man rode off.

"The child is nine years old! Do you fear he will attack me?" exclaimed Artor.

"He is a fox kit. I am afraid you will love him, and be hurt when he goes back to his wild kin. . . ."

Artor shut his lips, remembering the incident Cai referred to. He was grateful that his foster-brother had not mentioned Oesc, whom he had also made his hostage, and loved, and at Mons Badonicus been forced to kill. *His* little son must be almost eight by now.

He shook off the memory as Goriat returned, the frowning child kicking his pony to keep up with him. Despite his Saxon name, Ceawlin had the look of the Belgic royal house from whom his grandfather Ceretic had come.

Our blood is already mingling, thought Artor. *How long before we will be one in spirit?* He thought once more of the other little boy, Oesc's son, whose mother was Britannic and royal as well.

"Are you enjoying the journey?"

The grey glance flickered swiftly upward, then Ceawlin fixed his gaze on the road once more.

"You will have seen more of Britannia by now than any of the boys at home." Artor saw the frown began to ease and hid a smile. "But perhaps you miss the southern lands. It is in my mind to send you to stay at Camalot, under the care of my queen."

"Does she have a little boy?"

Artor twitched, momentarily astonished that the question should bring such pain. But Ceawlin could have no idea he had even struck a blow, much less how near to the bone. Would Guendivar learn to love this fox kit he was sending her? Or would she weep in secret because her husband had not been able to give her a child?

Goriat was telling the boy about Camalot, where the children of the folk who cooked and kept the livestock and stood guard ran laughing along the walls. The princes and chieftains brought their sons when they came visiting, but they were all British. At least Oesc had had Cunorix and Betiver as companions.

"Perhaps we will send for Eormenric of Cantuware to keep you company—" he said then. "Would you like that?"

Ceawlin nodded. "His father was my grandfather's ally."

Cai raised an eyebrow. This kit was not going to be easy to tame.

Eormenric had been raised by his mother to be Artor's friend. Still, he would need friends among the Saxons as well, and perhaps Ceawlin would be more willing to listen to another boy. They could guard each other's backs against the British child-pack, and Guendivar would win them over as she did everyone.

Artor closed his eyes for a moment, seeing against his eyelids the gleam of her amber hair. When he was at home, the knowledge of how he had failed her was sometimes so painful he longed to be away. But when he was far from her, Guendivar haunted his dreams.

"That is settled, then," he said briskly. "Goriat, I will give you an escort to take the boy south, and letters to the queen." Then, as the young man looked mutinous, "Do not fear for my safety—Cai here will be suspicious enough for two. Besides, was there not some story that the Picts wanted you to husband one of their princesses? I fear to let them set eyes on you!"

At the blush that suffused Goriat's cheeks everyone began to laugh, and Artor knew that his nephew would not dare to protest again.

Two more days of travel brought them a glimpse of bright water to the east, where the estuary of the Bodotria cut deeply into the land. Here their ways parted, Goriat and his men to continue on to Dun Eidyn and then south with the boy, and Artor and his party north to seek the headwaters of the Tava and the Pictish clanholds of Fodreu.

*   *   *

"Goriat was right! The fair weather didn't last," grumbled Cai. "Damn this Devil's murk—how are we to see our road?"

Artor wiped rain from his eyes and peered ahead. The weather had closed in as predicted, and all day they had travelled through a drizzling rain. If they had not come so far already, he might have been tempted to turn around, but at this point he judged them close to Fodreu. If they could find it, he thought gloomily. But they were as likely to get lost going back as keeping on. He could only hope that the Picts kept a good watch on their hunting runs, and would guide them in.

The track they followed wound between rolling hills. From time to time he glimpsed above them the shadows of higher mountains, as if they had been conjured from the mists for a moment, only to vanish away. *Merlin could conjure them back again*, he thought wistfully. *I wish Merlin were here.*

The black horse stumbled on the rocky path and instinctively he tightened the rein, sending reassurance with knees and hands. Raven collected himself and began, more carefully, to move once more. Artor shifted position on the saddle, whose hard frame was beginning to chafe through the damp leather breeches. The superb steel of his sword, kept oiled and clean, would be all right, but it seemed to him that the lesser metal of his mail shirt, inherited from some barbarian auxiliary, was beginning to rust already.

Another few steps and the black horse checked again, head up and nostrils flaring.

"It's all right, old boy—" The king leaned forward to pat the damp neck, and stilled as the humped shapes of shrub and boulder on the hillside ahead of them began to move. Dim figures of men on shaggy ponies seemed to emerge from the hill.

Someone shouted a warning, and Cai kicked his mount forward to cover the king, sword hissing from its sheath. He was swearing softly. Artor himself straightened, reaching for the hilt of his own blade. Then he paused. Why weren't they yelling? And why had there been no preliminary flight of arrows to cut the Britons down?

Behind him his own men were frantically struggling to string their bows. Artor lifted one hand. "Wait!"

Quivering with tension, the Britons stared as the Pictish riders emerged from the mist. They rode swathed in lengths of heavy cloth striped and chequered in the natural colors of the wool, to which the moisture beaded and clung. As they came closer, Artor noted that they smelled like sheep too.

The first riders were small men, wild haired and heavily bearded, but they drew aside for another, tall as a Briton, with the gold torque of a chieftain glinting from beneath his plaid. He halted his pony without appearing to signal and surveyed the strangers from beneath bent brows.

"Who is leader of the southern men?" His accent was odd, but his speech clear enough.

The king moved out from behind Cai, hand still lifted in the sign of peace. "It is I, Artor of Britannia. We seek the dun of Drest Gurthinmoch, King of all the Picts. Can you take us there?"

The Pictish chieftain nodded. "He sent us to find you. Fire and food are waiting, and"—his lips twitched beneath the russet mustache—"dry clothes."

That night, as he sat drinking heather ale at the Pict-king's fire, Artor reflected that Drest Gurthinmoch's hospitality was certainly preferable to his hostility. Artor's stiffening muscles made movement painful, but a good fire and a full belly more than compensated. And above all, he was glad, as the Pictish chieftain had promised, to be dry.

Overhead the peak of the thatched roof rose to unknown distances behind the smoke that veiled it, but at the level of the fire the air was clear. Artor had seen roundhouses in the western parts of Britannia, but never one of such size. In Roman lands, princes preferred the elegant villas, plastered and painted, of the conqueror. The roundhouse that formed the center of King Drest's dun was nearly as wide as the basilica in Calleva, its concentric uprights carved and painted with zig-zags, crescents and circles and the abstract renderings of boar and salmon, bull and horse and bird that he took to be the totems of the Pictish clans.

My ancestors lived like this before the Romans came . . . Artor thought then. He felt as if he had gone into a faerie hill where time ran backwards, returning him to the past.

King Drest was speaking. Artor turned, cupping one ear as if it was the noise, and not his own abstraction, that had made him miss the Pict-king's words.

"It is good my men found you," said Drest in his gutteral accent. The speech of the Pict-lords was as old-fashioned as their hall, a Brythonic dialect mixed with other words from a language he did not know.

"Truly—" Artor replied. "It was ill weather to be out on the moors."

"Ach—'tis of another danger I'd be warning you," the Pict replied. "There are worse things than weather, or even the wild beasts that haunt the hills."

His voice had lowered to a conspiratorial whisper and Artor leaned back, brows lifting, sensing a story.

"You'd not be likely to meet Bloody Comb, now, riding in a large and well-armed company. But he's a fearsome sight to a lone traveler, with his red eyes and his talon nails."

"And a bloody head?"

Drest grimaced. "It is the head of the traveler that grows bloody, when the creature has pelted him with heavy stones, and carries off the blood in his cap to feed."

"Bloody Comb is fearsome," said one of his chieftains, grinning, "but the Hidden People are more dangerous, they that live under the hills."

"It is because they look like men," a big man with fair hair put in. "But old age does not touch them. They steal our women, and change their sickly babes for our own."

"Do they have treasure?" asked Artor, remembering some of the tales he had heard. These stories were known everywhere, though the fair folk seemed to dwindle in the Roman lands.

"Surely, for they have been here since the first mothers of our folk came into this land. They are creatures of night and shadow, but they grow weak and ugly if you catch them in the full light of day. You can kill them then with ease."

"And they would liefer die than reveal where their treasure

is hid," said the chieftain. "Like the female we caught two moons past. She screamed, but would say nothing until she died."

Artor looked away, trying not to imagine the treatment that had made the woman, whatever she was, scream. Suddenly the barbaric splendor of Drest Gurthinmoch's dun seemed less attractive. And yet he had to admit that many Romans, if they had believed in the treasure at all, might have done the same.

"I see that I have had a narrow escape," he said in a neutral tone, "and bless the fate that led me to Drest Gurthinmoch's dun. If I had known your hospitality was so generous, I would have come before. . . ."

Without a sword in your hand? The echo of his words showed clearly in the sardonic gleam of the Pict-king's eyes.

"If there has been less than friendship between your people and mine, it was not by my will—" Artor said quietly.

"Nor by mine—" his host agreed. "But we will speak more of that in the morning. For now, let you drink with me, and we shall see if the Britons can match the Pretani as well at the ale-vats as they do on the battlefield!" He began to laugh.

Artor awoke with a throbbing head. When he staggered out to the horse trough he saw that it was well past dawn. His memories of the preceding evening were chaotic, culminating in a tide of boozy good fellowship that had borne him to his bed. *I hope I may not have sworn away half Britannia . . . what do they put in their beer?*

By the time he had doused his head in the chill water, he was feeling less like a victim of Bloody Comb, and could greet Drest Gurthinmoch, stout, ruddy, and apparently unaffected by the night's carouse, without wincing as his own words echoed against his skull.

"Come," said the Pict, "we will walk, and complete your cure in the sweet air."

Artor grimaced. His condition must be more obvious than he had thought. Still it was a good suggestion, and as movement worked the stiffness out of his muscles, he began to feel more like a man, if not yet entirely like a king.

The royal dun lay on the shore of the Tava, which here ran deep and smoothly between two lines of hills. Beyond the great feasting hall lay the house of the queen, its thatching dyed in patterns of dull red and green and blue. The gate to the palisade was open, and in the meadow horses and cattle were grazing. At first Artor thought he had been brought out here to admire them, but the Pict-king led him along a path that led towards the trees. Seeing the noble stand of oaks that rose before him, Artor understood that he was being taken to the *nemeton* of the tribe.

The meadow had been full of sounds—the whicker of a pony and the stamp of hooves, bee song, and the twitter of birds—but the *nemeton* was very still. The whisper of wind in the upper leaves seemed to intensify the silence below. As they came to the edge of the clearing, Artor felt a change in pressure and stopped short.

Drest Gurthinmoch turned back, smiling. "Ah, you feel it? That is well, but the guardians will allow you to enter, since you are with me." He reached out, and after a moment Artor grasped his hand.

For a moment the shift dizzied him; then he was in, surrounded by trees that seemed to watch him like the standing stones at the Giant's Dance. And in the center of this circle there also lay a stone.

"The king stone . . ." said the Pict. "When I stood upon it at my king-making, it cried out, for those who know how to hear. Do you not have the custom in your land?"

Artor considered the chunk of sandstone, a rough rectangle of a height for a man to sit on, with an indentation that might have been a footprint on its upper side. In the north, he knew, every tribe had its navel stone, the focus of gatherings. There were sacred stones in Britannia as well, but where the Romans ruled, their use had been forgotten.

"No longer—" he whispered.

"I come here when I need to think like a king. . . ." Drest motioned him to sit beside him on the fallen log that lay at the edge of the clearing. "Why do you want to cross the narrow sea?"

The sudden question took Artor by surprise. No point in

asking the old wolf how he knew it—no doubt he had an informant in Artor's household just as there were men in Pict-land who carried news to the British king.

"To fight the Franks," he said at last.

"Why? They do not raid your shores."

"Not yet. But they are hungry. One day, like the Romans, they will cross the sea. Better to stop them now than wait until they are in our hunting runs—or yours."

Drest looked thoughtful. "So this war that you go to will defend us as well?"

"That is what I believe." Artor was thinking, he realized, like a Roman, who had protected their borders by conquering what lay beyond them. But the Romans had not known when to stop. He would be wiser.

The Pict-king grunted. "Then I will guard your back."

Artor sat up, skin flushing with the release from tension he had not known he carried until now.

"Blood seals an alliance better than breath," Drest said then. "It is a pity that you have no child."

I have a son. . . . Medraut's face sprang suddenly to mind, but Artor kept silent.

"One of your sister's sons will be your heir, as is right, but she bore several. It would be well if one of them could be sent here to wed one of our royal women." He looked at Artor slyly. "One day your blood might rule the Pretani after all . . ."

Artor licked dry lips. "They are grown men. I . . . cannot choose for them. But I will ask."

"Or a man of your Companions, though my people will not see that as so binding. Still, they would value for his own sake any man trained in your war-band."

Artor's lips twitched at the compliment. "I will ask."

The Britons took care to delay their departure until the sun returned, but Artor was fast learning that the weather this far north could never be relied on. By the time they reached the firth, a chill wind was gusting in from the sea, driving dark clouds that trailed veils of rain. He only hoped that the Picts were more trustworthy than the sky.

Across the firth he could see in silhouette the Rock of Dun Eidyn, stark against the clouds. But the water between frothed with foam. Clearly no boat would ply those seas until the wind died down. The king halted his black horse at the edge of the sand, gazing across the heaving waves with a longing that surprised him. He wanted to be back in his own country!

Cai was saying something about a wood in whose shelter they could wait out the storm, but Artor shook his head.

"I've never liked boats anyway," he said crossly. "We'll ride east, go around."

Cai shook his head gloomily, but he turned away and began to give the necessary orders all the same. The king felt a moment's compunction—he knew that the knee his foster-brother had injured at Mons Badonicus gave him trouble in wet weather, but no doubt it would ache as much sitting still in a damp forest as on the trail.

Yet for a time it seemed that Artor's decision had been a good one. Away from the sea the storm's strength lessened, and the rain diminished to a drizzle as night drew near. Their campsite was damp, but even when wet, the lengths of tightly woven natural wool that King Drest had given them to use as riding cloaks stayed warm.

In the morning the air seemed warmer, and the rain had almost ceased, but before they had been an hour on the trail they wished it back again, for the rain-soaked earth was giving up its moisture in the form of fog. Heavy and clinging, it weighted the lungs and penetrated to the bone. A trackway seemed to lead away to the right; they turned their mounts uphill, hoping to get above the fog and find shelter. The Picts who had escorted them knew the lay of the land, but none had the intimate local knowledge of each rock and tree that could have guided them now.

The mist deadened sound. They had dismounted, and Artor could hear the clop and scrape behind him as Raven picked his way over mud and stone. The sounds of the other horses came faintly, and as darkness fell, their shapes faded to shadows more sensed than seen. Something loomed ahead and the black horse threw up his head, snorting in alarm.

Artor pulled him down, stroking the sweated neck to soothe him. It was only a big boulder, though in the half-dark it humped like a crouching beast. He led Raven around it, and pulled him gently after the receding shape of the horse ahead of him.

Or at least that was what he thought he was doing. He had walked for perhaps as long as it takes to boil an egg before he realized that the figure he thought he was following was another boulder. He paused, listening. The heavy whuff of Raven's breathing was the only sound.

For a moment the king stood and swore. Then he fumbled for the strap that held his horn. He set it to his lips and blew, the sound dull in the heavy air. From somewhere above him came an answer. Artor loosened the rein and the horse started forward.

Three more times after that he blew the horn, and each time the reply came more faintly, until he could hear nothing at all. It was full dark now, and if he wandered further, he risked damaging the horse's legs in some unseen hole. The ground was rising. He stubbed his toe on a large stone and stepped aside, finding more even ground beyond it. His mount stopped short, trembling, and Artor yanked on the rein. Even in the thick air he noticed the shift in pressure that told him the rock he had just passed had been no ordinary boulder, but by now he scarcely cared. If the place made the horse nervous, perhaps wild creatures would avoid it. In any case, he could go no further now.

He hobbled the horse by feel and removed the bridle, un-girthed the saddle pad and laid it on the ground next to an upended slab of stone. Another slab lay half over it, and he pulled the pad beneath it, grateful for whatever protection it might afford. Then, wrapping the Pictish plaid around him, he lay down.

It was warmer than he had expected in the shelter of the stones. He felt pieces of something like broken pottery beneath the blanket and swept them aside. Fragments of warning tugged at his memory, but exhaustion was already overwhelming him. He was asleep before he could decide whether he ought to be afraid.

*   *   *

"Artor . . . Defender of Britannia . . . arise. . . ."

Blinking, the king sat up. He was glad to wake from the old nightmare about Mons Badonicus, but as he stared around him he wondered if he had passed into another dream. It was still night, but there was no mist within the circle, and the stones glowed. In their eerie light he saw that his shelter consisted of a slab of rock balanced on two others like a small table, but instead of the bare earth he expected beneath it, he saw a lighted tunnel that led down into the hill.

"Artor, come to Me. . . ."

The king glanced swiftly around him. His horse stood hip-slung, head low in sleep. The call was coming from the depths. A whisper from his waking mind warned him not to answer, but the voice was sweet as his mother's croon, golden as Guendivar's laughter. No mortal could have resisted that call.

He knelt, peering into the opening. And it seemed to him that the space grew larger, or perhaps it was he who was becoming small, for what he saw now was a tunnel through which he could walk easily.

The light flared before him. When he could see once more, he found himself in a round chamber carved out of the rock. He could not see the passage through which he had entered, and there were people all around him. With a start of of pure terror, he understood that the Hidden People had him in their power.

Artor took a deep breath and looked around him. They did not seem hostile. Men and women stared back at him. They had the look of some of the men he had seen among the Picts, sturdy of body with grey eyes and thick-springing earth-brown hair, but they were not dressed like anyone he had ever seen. Warriors went bare-chested, their loins wrapped in woolen kilts held by belts ornamented with plaques of gold. Their skin was blue with tattooed designs, and at their sides hung leaf-shaped bronze swords. Other men wore the skins of beasts, clasped on one shoulder. There were women in gathered skirts and shawls, their hair coiled in netted caps, while others wore a single garment held at the shoulders with brooches of bronze or gold.

They had wealth enough, whoever they were—gold at wrist and ear, and crescent necklets of beaten gold. As he wondered, the crowd parted and a man robed in white wool appeared. He had a look of Merlin, but he was smaller, his breast and shoulders sheathed in gold. An imperious gesture summoned Artor, and the people drew back, pointing at his mail shirt and his sword.

At the back of the cave a woman sat throned on an out-cropping of stone. There were carvings on it; he realized that the entire cavern was carved in spirals so that its contours blurred. But he had no attention to spare for them now. Those same spirals twined across the ivory flesh of the woman's bare torso—no, not merely a woman, he thought as he noted the diadem of gold that gleamed from the cloud of dark hair—a queen. She was very like Drest Gurthinmoch's woman whom the Picts called the Great Mare. A skirt of painted linen fell in stiff folds beneath her belly; for mantle she had the thick furs of forest cats, the wicked heads drawn over her shoulders. Cairngorms glinted from their slanted eyes.

"Defender. . . ."

Unbidden, Artor fell to his knees. Her eyes, too, were like those of the Pictish queen.

"What do you want of me?" His voice was harsh in his own ears.

"Defend this land—"

"I have done so since I was fifteen winters old."

"Defend your people," the queen said then. "All of them—the children of the earth-folk as well as the children of the sun."

Artor set his hand on the pommel of his sword. "I am pledged to deal justly with all those who dwell in this hal-lowed isle."

"Men need not justice only, but hope, and a dream." Her voice was harsh honey.

Artor shook his head. "How can I give them that, Lady? I am only a man. . . ."

"You are the child of the Bear, you are the Raven of Britannia," she continued implacably. "Are you willing to become her eternal king?"

Artor remembered the oaths he had sworn at his anointing. But this was something different, a bright shadow on the soul. As he hesitated, she spoke again.

"There is a price to be paid."

"What do you want?"

"Touch the Stone, and you will understand."

For a long moment he stared at her. "Where shall I find it?" he whispered at last.

Her eyes held his, and his head began to swim. "It is here . . ." The stone on which she was sitting began to glow. As Artor reached towards it her words were echoed from all around him: "Here . . . here . . . HERE!"

The blaze became blinding and he fell into light.

Artor awakened to a sharp and localized pain just above his breastbone. His eyes opened, and he became very still. Beneath his nose he glimpsed the dull gleam of a flint spearhead. His gaze followed the shaft to the man who held it. For a moment he thought he was still dreaming, for the spearman was stocky, with a brown bush of hair like the warriors he had seen in the cavern. Then he realized that this man was weathered, his hide cape tattered with wear. He was not alone.

"Who are you?" one of the other men asked in guttural Brythonic. He was a little better dressed than the others, but Artor recognized his captors as the people of the hills against whom the Pict-lords had warned him. But he knew them now for the first inhabitants of this land. One of the strangers held Raven by the bridle. The black horse stamped and shook his head, but did not try to get away.

Moving very slowly, the king edged away from under the spear and sat up, brushing more potsherds away as he set down his hand. Someone gasped and made a sign of warding.

"I am the Defender of Britannia . . ." he answered, his mind still filled with echoes of his dream.

"You are here all night?"

Artor nodded. The sky was still grey, but the mist no longer hugged the hills. A light wind gave hope that it might clear later in the day.

"I was lost in the mist." He looked around him, only now appreciating the strangeness of his refuge. "This place seemed . . . warm."

"You sleep with the Old Ones. . . ." The speaker showed broken teeth in a grim smile. "This is their tomb."

Artor looked around him at the kerb of stones and the megaliths in whose shelter he had lain, understanding now the nervousness with which they eyed him.

"I am a living man."

The speaker reached out and gripped his shoulder. "He is solid," he confirmed.

"I feel hollow—" Artor added with a smile. "I have not eaten since yestermorn."

"We kill strangers who come into our hunting runs—do the children of the Great Mare not tell you so?" the first man said bitterly.

Artor drew up his knees and rested his arms upon them, knowing it would be fatal to show himself afraid. "If your ancestors did not take my soul, it is not for you to do so."

The speaker muttered to the others then turned back again. "I know you. You are the one they call the Bear, the lord of the sun-people beyond the Wall."

"I am he." Artor nodded, wondering if admitting it was wise. But he found himself compelled to speak truth here.

"Come—it is not well to stay in a place of the old ones, even by day. We give you food and lead you to your men. We watch them since sunset past, but they do not see us there." The grim smile flickered again. "But there is a price."

"There is always a price—" said Artor, remembering his vision of the night. "Name it."

"Speak for us to the children of the Great Mare. They drive us from the best lands already. Let them leave us alone, not hunt us like deer."

Artor looked at them, noting bad teeth and thinning hair, legs bowed with malnutrition. Saxon and Roman, Briton and Pict alike were newcomers next to these, the original inhabitants of Britannia. Slowly he got to his feet and set his hand on the pommel of the Chalybe sword.

"Will you take me as your king?"

The speaker looked him up and down, then grinned. "By star and stone we swear it."

"Then by star and stone I will swear also to protect you."

†HE ORCHARD

A·D· 504

Artor walked with his mother by the Lake, where the apple orchard came down to the shore. Igierne used a cane now, and paused often to catch her breath. It was clear that movement was painful, but she had refused to stop, nor did she complain. When they came to the long rock that had been shaped roughly into a seat she eased down with a sigh.

He stood behind her, one hand resting lightly on her thin shoulder. Trees circled the lake and clung to the lower slopes of the hills, dark masses of evergreen mingled with bare branches just showing the first haze of spring green. On the apple trees, buds were swelling, their branches framing the shining silver water and the shaded masses of surrounding hills that held the lake like a cup in their strong hands.

Here the bones of the earth showed strong and clear. In the mountains Artor found an enduring beauty for which the changing displays of leaf and flower were only an adornment—like his mother, he thought, whose fine bone structure retained its beauty despite the softly wrinkled skin.

"It is beautiful," Igierne said softly. "It is worth the labor of getting here for the refreshment of spirit it brings."

"I might say the same," answered the king. He had spent

much of the winter with Cunobelinus at Trimontium, and seen him sworn king over the Votadini on the stone at the base of its hill, and at the moment the chieftain's foot touched the stone, Artor had heard the earth's exultant cry.

From there he had travelled down the eastern coast. He was glad now that he had decided to follow the old Roman Wall west again to the Isle of Maidens. Since the last time he had seen her, his mother had grown visibly more frail.

"Look—" She pointed towards the eastern hills. "There is the path that leads up to the circle of stones."

"I stopped there on my way," said Artor, remembering the ring of stones. Some had fallen, and the tallest were no more than breast high, as if the earth were slowly reclaiming a broken crown. "How many are there? I counted three times and the answer was never the same."

"Ah, that secret belongs to our Mysteries—"

Artor shook his head, laughing. "Is that why those stones are so—*alive*? Most of the circles I have seen are somnolent as an old dog in the sun. But the ones on the hill hummed with energy."

"And how would you know that?" Igierne turned to look up at him.

Artor kept his gaze on the hills. "Because I have met the folk who built them. Or their spirits. I wish I had thought to ask them *why*!"

"Tell me—" Igierne's voice changed, and Artor knew that she was speaking as Lady of the Lake. Easing down beside her, he began to describe the night he had spent beneath the ancient stones.

"And now," he ended, "it is as if I were growing new senses. I can tell, before I even touch it, if a stone has weathered naturally or was shaped by the Old Ones of this land. Who was the Lady I saw, and what did her question mean?"

"I would guess . . . she was a great queen of the elder days, so bound to the land that after her death she would not pass onward to the Blessed Isles, but became one with the spirits of the earth. To some . . ." she spoke ever more slowly, "that choice is given. They become part of the Otherworld that lies like a veil above our own. In some places the fabric is folded, and there, the two worlds touch."

"That grave was one of them . . ." he said slowly. "As are all the places where the old ones worked the stones. . . ."

"In their proper times and seasons, it is so."

Artor realized that he was gripping the rock on which he sat. Beneath his palm its chill surface was warming; he felt a vibration as if some great beast purred beneath his hand, and let go quickly.

"What is the price? And where is the Stone? The Votadini king stone belongs to that land and that people only. Where is the Stone that will hail me as king and emperor?"

Igierne shook her head. "That is *your* mystery." She looked at him again. "Why do you want to be emperor? Is it the old dream of glory that draws you—the need to avenge Maximian?"

"Perhaps it was . . . at first," he replied. "I admit that Riothamus' offer was flattering. But I have been thinking about it as I travelled around this land. The Lady commanded me to defend all the races who dwell in Britannia, from the earthfolk to the Saxons. At its best, the justice of Rome did that, but the Pax Romana has failed."

"Will you impose a Pax Britannica upon the world?"

"Perhaps, to keep this Island safe, that is what I will have to do. . . ."

Igierne sighed. "You have seen the tumbled stones of the second wall that the Romans built to defend the first one that Hadrianus made. Each conquest only gave them a new land that had to be protected. But in the end they could not hold all they had taken. To be accepted by all of Britannia is more than any other prince of our people has achieved—do you truly believe that you can be a king for Gallia as well?"

"Mother, I do not know. But to bring peace to the world and justice to its peoples, we need a dream. I think I have to try. . . ."

Morgause was in the weaving shed, supervising the younger priestesses as they checked the bags of raw fleece, when she realized that someone was standing in the doorway. She looked up, eyes narrowed against the glare. For a moment he was only a shape outlined in light; then she recognized the broad shoulders and height of the king. Slowly she straightened. For the three days of Artor's visit she had managed to avoid him, but there was no evading a confrontation now.

"Verica, I must go—make sure that any bags that have gotten moths in them over the winter are taken to the other shed. If we wash the fleeces thoroughly, we may be able to save some of the wool."

The younger priestess nodded, and Morgause made her way past the women to the door.

"Ah—" Artor essayed a smile. "I am glad you came out to me. I would rather charge a Saxon army than intrude on all those chattering girls."

"Truly? I thought there was nothing you would not dare—" Morgause fought to keep her tone even.

Artor shook his head. "Will you walk with me? We need to speak about Medraut." Together, they moved down the path.

"What has he done?"

"Why should you ask that? Was he so difficult a child to raise?" Artor asked quickly.

Not at all. Not until the last. . . . Morgause pulled her shawl more tightly around her, for clouds were gathering, pushed by a chilly wind. "Your tone suggested he was in trouble . . ." she said aloud.

"On the way north there were . . . accidents. I sent Medraut to the Saxons—to Cynric at Venta Belgarum, who for the sake of his own cub's life will guard him as the apple of his eye. It would seem that the secret of Medraut's parentage has become known, and perhaps there are some who think they would be doing me a favor to get rid of him."

"Perhaps they are right," Morgause answered bitterly. "Why should you trust him, when he is what I made him? You have good reason to distrust *me.*"

"For the Lady's sake, Morgause! It may be that he should never have been born, but he is here, and he deserves a chance. I have not come here to blame you, but you know him better than anyone else. Like it or not, he is my son. I need to understand. . . ."

Morgause stared up at the brother she had hated so long and so intimately betrayed. He was still strong, but there was silver in the brown hair, and his face was carved by lines of responsibility and power. He seemed so sure of himself, as if he had never doubted his own integrity, that she almost began to hate him once more.

Should I tell him that Medraut is brilliant and seductive and dangerous? How much am I willing to admit? How much do I dare? Looking back, the woman who had manipulated and schemed seemed like a stranger, but the reverberations of that woman's past actions still troubled the present, like the ripples from a cast stone.

"Medraut is very intelligent," she said slowly, shame moderating her words. "But his brothers were too much older—he has been very much alone. He does not have much experience of friendship." She paused. "I raised him to think he had a right to your throne."

"That is the one thing I cannot give him," Artor replied, his gaze troubled. "Even if his birth were acceptable, what I have to leave will go to the man best fitted to hold it. To the man, if there is one, who is chosen by the spirit of this Sword. I told him that. I do not know if he believed me—" he said then, gripping the hilt of the weapon that hung at his side.

"Then you must somehow teach him to be worthy of it," said Morgause, "for that is what he will desire."

Perhaps, she thought, *in rejecting me, Medraut will reject what I taught him.* But she found that hard to believe.

Artor was staring out across the lake, his gaze as grey as the troubled surface of the water.

"One thing I would ask of you—" she said aloud. "To take Gualchmai's daughter with you when you go. She is a wild creature of the moors, not suited by nature for the quiet life we have here. Perhaps Guendivar will be able to tame her."

"Very well. What is her name?"

"She is called Ninive."

* * *

At the feast of Christ's Resurrection, the queen and her household journeyed from Camalot to the Isle of Afallon to hear mass at the round church there. Sister Julia was here, having finally taken full vows as a nun, but to Guendivar, it was as if she walked with the ghost of the girl she had once been. Here, Queen Igierne had set her on the path to her destiny. And now she was woman and queen, but not a mother.

Men were beginning to whisper that that strange boy, Medraut, was Artor's son. It seemed to Guendivar that they looked on her less kindly now, holding her a barren stock and no true queen. *But even the most fertile field will not bear without sowing,* she thought bitterly. If she was at fault, it was not because she could not conceive, but because she had not been able to awaken the manhood of the king.

When the service was over, Guendivar walked out of its scented darkness and stood blinking in the sunshine. On this day, the Church forgot its mysteries of blood and sorrow and rejoiced in life reborn, and the world seemed to echo that joy. Above the smooth peak of the Tor, the clouds from last night's storm hung white and fluffy in a blue sky.

The wind was chilly enough for her cloak to be welcome, but there was a promise of warming weather in the heat of the sun. She could not waste such a day cooped up with a flock of chattering women—but she glimpsed two small heads, one red, one fair, by the horse trough, and began to smile.

"Ceawlin! Eormenric! Come walk with me!" she called.

"Oh my lady, wait—" Netta, the woman who tended the boys, came bustling over. "The wretched children have soaked each other with their splashing and must have dry things!"

Eormenric shook himself like a puppy and Ceawlin looked mutinous as Guendivar bent to touch the cloth.

"They are a little damp, truly, but the day is growing warmer. They will dry off soon enough if they run about in the sun!" She turned to the boys. "Will you escort me, my warriors? I would walk in the orchard for awhile."

Yipping gleefully, they dashed ahead, then circled back

around her. Fox-red Ceawlin had the features of his Belgic forebears, but in thought and speech he was all Saxon. It was Eormenric, in appearance a lanky, blond reincarnation of Oesc, his father, who was most fluent in the British tongue and easy with their ways. That was the doing of Rigana, who had been born a princess of Cantium and now was Cantuware's queen. Artor had been wise to ask her to send her son to Camalot. The boys had become fast friends.

The apple trees were leafing out, with only a few flowered branches remaining to bear witness to their former snowy glory. Guendivar had pulled one down to smell the scent when she heard a cry behind her.

Ceawlin lay sprawled on the grass, like a doll dropped by some child in play. Eormenric bent over him, then straightened, gazing at Guendivar in mute appeal.

"He fell out of the tree—"

Guendivar knelt. She could feel her own heart thumping alarm as she felt at his throat for the pulse that beat in answer to her own.

"Did he fall on his head?" she asked, sitting back on her heels.

"I think so—" answered Eormenric. "Is he going to die?"

"Not today," she said, hoping it was true. "But he will have a sore head when he wakes up." Carefully she felt his limbs.

Ceawlin stirred, whimpering. "*Modor....*"

It needed no knowledge of Saxon to interpret that. Guendivar settled herself with her back to the tree trunk and gathered the boy against her breast. For a moment she remembered how the priest had wept over the image of Christ's mother with her dead son in her arms. But this boy would not die—she would not allow it! She tightened her grip on Ceawlin, and as naturally as a puppy, Eormenric snuggled beneath her other arm.

"It will be all right," she murmured. "All will be well...."

The tree at her back was a steady support, the scent of crushed grass intoxicating. Guendivar leaned into its strength, and suddenly it seemed to her as if she had become the tree, rooting herself in the awakening earth and drawing up strength through her spine. Power welled through her from the depths of the earth to the child in her arms.

Ceawlin stirred again, and this time when his eyes opened there was recognition in his gaze. She waited for him to tense and pull away, but he only sighed and burrowed more comfortably against her.

She steadied her breathing, willing the shift in vision that would show her the spirits of the apple trees. The world began to change around her, but the shift was going too fast. Held in this moment, she went deeper than ever before. She *was* the solid earth and the warmth of the sunlight, the wind that stirred her hair and the pliant strength of the tree, a woman's body and the children in her arms, all part of a single whole. Life was reborn from the womb of earth with the springtime as the Christian god came forth from his earthen tomb. And in that moment, Guendivar understood that she was not barren at all.

She did not count the passing of time, but surely the sun had not moved far across the sky when she became aware that someone was speaking. For a time she simply listened to the musical rise and fall of the language, for it was a tongue she did not know. The sound seemed to come from all around her, as if the wind were speaking in the leaves.

> *"Come to the holy temple of the virgins*
> *Where the pleasant grove of apple trees*
> *Circles an altar smoking with frankincense."*

The words became more distinct, and she realized that now she was hearing the British tongue.

> *"The roses leave shadow on the ground*
> *And cool springs murmur through apple branches*
> *Where shuddering leaves pour down profound sleep."*

It must be true, thought Guendivar, for Ceawlin, eyes closed and breathing even, had passed into a healing slumber, and even Eormenric lay quiet against her breast. But her expanded soul was returning to the confines of her body. She heard with her mortal senses, therefore the words she was hearing must have some tangible source.

"In that meadow where horses have grown glossy,
And all spring flowers grow wild,
The anise shoots fill the air with aroma."

She straightened a little, turning her head, and saw a man, his limbs as gnarled and brown as the branches, sitting in one of the apple trees. In that first moment, the sight seemed quite normal, as if he had grown there. And so she was not startled when returning awareness resolved the abstract pattern of bearded face and skin-clad body into the figure of Merlin.

Seeing her gaze upon him, the Druid slid down from the tree and took up the staff that had been leaning against it.

"And there our queen Aphrodite pours
Celestial nectar in the gold cups,
Which she fills gracefully with sudden joy."

"Heathen words . . ." Guendivar said softly, "for such a holy day."

"Holy words, first sung for the Goddess by a lovely lady in the Grecian isles. In those days it was the death of Her lover Attis that the women mourned in the spring. The gods die and are reborn, but the Goddess, like the earth, is eternal. You know this to be true—I see the understanding in your eyes." Merlin came closer and squatted on his haunches, the staff leaning against his shoulder.

"Perhaps . . . but I am no goddess, to be hailed with such words."

"Are you not?" He laughed softly. "At least you are Her image, sitting there with your sons in your arms."

Guendivar looked at him in alarm, remembering the sense of union she had experienced only a few moments ago. How could the old man know what she was feeling? The last time he had tried to talk to her she had run from him, but she could not disturb the sleeping boys.

"And you are Her image to your husband's warriors, their Lady and Queen."

"But not to my husband," Guendivar said bitterly.

"All things change, even he, even you. Is it not so?"

"Even you?" she asked then.

He laughed softly, long fingers stroking lightly over the staff that lay against his arm. Its head was swathed in yellowed linen, but she could see now that strange symbols were carved up and down the shaft.

"I have been a salmon in the stream and a stag upon the hill. I have been an acorn in the forest, and the falcon floating in the wind. I was an old man once, but now I am as young as the cub just born this spring. . . ."

It was true, she thought. He had not moved like an old man, though the hair that covered his body was grizzled as a wolf's pelt, and streaks of pure silver glinted in his hair and beard.

"I think sometimes that I will be old without ever having seen my prime, passing directly from virginity to senility . . ." Guendivar said then.

"Do you believe that to bear in the body is the only fertility? I was a father to Artor, though another man begot him. It is not what you receive, but what you give, that will grant you fulfillment. You must become a conduit for power."

Ceawlin stirred, and she soothed him with a gentle touch. "How?" she asked when the boy had settled once more.

"You have done it already, when you brought the earth power through the tree. Build up an image of the Lady of Life standing behind you, and you will become a doorway through which Her force can flow."

Did she dare to believe it might be so? She would have questioned him further, but Eormenric opened his eyes and seeing Merlin, sat up, staring. Ceawlin, disturbed by his motion, began to wake as well.

"What's *he* doing here?" whispered Eormenric.

"He is wise in all the ancient magics," Guendivar answered. "He will make sure that your friend is well. . . ."

And Merlin, taking his cue, rose in a single smooth motion and came to her, passing his hands above the boy's body and resting them on his brow. Ceawlin, who lay with eyes rolling like those of a frightened horse, whispered something in the Saxon tongue.

"What did he say?" Guendivar asked Eormenric.

"He called the old man by the name of Woden and asked if he had come to take him to his hall . . ."

Merlin grunted and got to his feet. "Nay, child, I am a prophet sometimes, but no god." He stood looking down at the boy, his face growing grim. "I foresee for you a long life, and many victories."

His dark gaze lifted to meet hers, and Guendivar recoiled, wondering what it was he had seen. But without another word he turned and strode off and in a few moments had disappeared among the trees.

Guendivar stared after him. If he was not a god, she thought then, still, Merlin was something more than a man.

On a day of mingled sunlight and shadow towards the end of May, the high king of Britannia returned to Camalot. Another year's storms had weathered the timbers, and the thatching had been bleached by another year's suns to a paler gold. Artor remembered it half finished, all raw wood and pale stone, but now buildings and fortifications alike seemed to have grown out of the hill.

As always, he approached Camalot with mixed emotions. This was his home, the heart of his power, and here, in perpetual reminder of his greatest failure, was Guendivar. If he had been able to give her children, would she by now have grown fat and frowsy? But he had not, and so she remained in essence virgin, forever young, beautiful, and not to be possessed by any man.

Then they were passing beneath the gate, and the entire population of the fortress surged around him, obliterating thought in an ecstasy of welcome.

It was late that night before Artor and his queen were alone. He found himself grateful that the day had left him physically exhausted. Without the distracting demands of the body, it would be easier to remember the things he had to say.

Guendivar sat in her sleeping shift on the chest at the foot of their bed, combing out her hair. Long habit had taught him not to think of her with desire, but there were times when her beauty broke through his defenses.

She is a woman, he thought, his gaze lingering on the firm curves of breast and thigh, *no longer the green girl I took from her father's hall. A woman,* the thought went on, *who deserves better than I have been able to give. . . .*

He paused in his pacing and turned. "My lady, we need to talk—"

She picked up the comb again, features still half-veiled by the golden fall of her hair, but he sensed her attention. Her movement made the lamp flame flicker, sending a flurry of shadows across the woven hangings on the wall.

He cleared his throat. "I told you once that I had a son, but not by whom. I begot him on my sister, when I lay with her, all unknowing, at the rites of Lughnasa."

There was a charged silence, then the comb began to move once more.

"If you did not know, there was no sin—" Guendivar said slowly, then paused, thinking. "It is that boy Medraut, isn't it? The youngest son of Morgause who came to you last winter."

Artor nodded. "I hoped to keep his birth hidden, but the word has gotten around. It may be that he himself told someone the secret. Medraut can be. . . . strange."

"Do you wish to make him your heir?" she asked, frowning.

"Were he as good a man as Gualchmai, still the priests would never stand for it. Medraut cannot inherit, but men are saying . . . that his existence proves my fertility. Some of the chieftains came to me, suggesting that I should take another queen."

"Do you wish to divorce me?" Guendivar set down the comb and faced him, her eyes huge in a face drained of color.

"Guendivar—" Despite his will he could hear his voice shaking. "You know better than anyone that the fault lies in me. But it has come to me that by holding you to a barren bed I have wronged you. I thought things might have changed—in the North, I tried to take a girl, but I could do nothing. Morgause has repented, but she cannot alter the past. If you wish it, I will release you from the marriage, free you to find a man who can be a husband to you in fact as well as name."

She turned away and began once more, very slowly, to pull the ivory comb through her hair. "And if I do, and my new husband gets me with child, and men begin to say that the king has lost his manhood?"

"Be damned to them, so long as you are happy!" What was she thinking? He·wished he could see her eyes!

"Then be damned to those who say that I am sterile. I wish no other husband than you."

Artor had not known he was holding his breath until it rushed out of him in a long sigh. Guendivar set down the comb and began to braid the golden silk of her hair. Her gaze was on the long strands, but he could see the smooth curve of cheek and brow, and her beauty smote him like a sword. The leather straps that supported the mattress creaked as he sat down.

"And I . . . no other queen. . . ." He forced the words past a thickened throat.

Guendivar tied off her braid, blew out the lamp on her side of the bed, and climbed in.

"You have guarded my honor," he said then. "Now I ask you to guard Britannia. Except for Cataur, I have spoken with all of the princes. I will go to Dumnonia to gather ships, and my army will make the journey to Gallia. When I cross the sea, I want you to rule. I think my treaties will hold, but if they do not, I will leave you Gualchmai to lead the warriors, and Cai to handle the administration. Someone must make our proud princes work together. You have power over men, my queen. The authority will be yours."

Guendivar raised herself on one elbow. The light of the remaining lamp seemed to dance in her eyes. "You have given me those two Saxon cubs to raise already, and now you will give me a kingdom to rule?"

"I know of none other to whom I would entrust it," he said

slowly, shrugging off his chamber robe and tossing it to the foot of the bed.

"Then I will be the mother of many," she said softly, "and watch over the land until you return. But while you are still here, come to bed." She paused, and for a moment he thought she would say something more, but her gaze slid away from his, and she lay back down.

At the beginning of summer the Isca flowed calmly past the old capital of the Dumnonii. In the riverside meadow where the feasting tables had been arranged, a fresh wind was blowing up off the water, and though Artor could not see it, he thought he could smell the sea. He leaned back in the carved chair that once had graced the home of a Roman magistrate and took a deep breath, seeking the current of fresh air above the heavy scents of roasting meat and ale.

This campaign had been too long in the planning, but this summer, surely, he would see Gallia. On the plain above Portus Adurni his army was gathering even now. He had made all secure behind him. Only Dumnonia remained to settle, and the king was beginning to think that Cataur's country would be more trouble than the rest of Britannia combined.

"Do not be telling me that this campaign has nothing to do with you!" exclaimed Betiver, who had come back from Gallia to help with the final preparations. "In the North they provided men and horses, as I have heard, and they have far less reason to fear the Frankish power. I have been in Armorica, my friends, and I know well that half the country is ruled by princes from Dumnonia and Kernow. It is your own lands and kin we will be fighting for! The king expects you be to generous with ships and men."

Artor eyed Cataur, who sat at the other end of the long table, with a grim smile. The northerners might well think it worth the price to be out from under the king's eye for awhile, whereas the Dumnonians were unwilling to give up the independence they enjoyed across the sea. But that freedom from royal control was a luxury that they could no longer afford.

Cataur was shaking his head, complaining about bad harvests and hard times.

"The seasons have been no worse here than elsewhere," Artor put in suddenly, "and you never suffered from the Saxons. Even here in Isca you have found folk from Demetia to repopulate the town. You have the ships, and men who sail to Armorica every moon to steer them. And you shall have them back again once they have made a few voyages for me."

"Very well, that is fair enough." Abruptly Cataur capitulated, grinning through teeth gone bad with age. He had never really recovered from the wound he took in the last Saxon revolt, and his sons led his armies now.

"I will not ask you for more than a company of men," the king went on, "and your son Constantine to lead them. Together, we will raise more troops among your cousins in Armorica."

Cataur scowled at that, but Constantine was smiling. Not quite old enough to fight at Mons Badonicus, he had grown up on tales of the heroes of the Saxon wars. Artor suspected he regretted never having had a chance to win his own glory. Long ago Cataur had been a contender for the kingship, and Constantine, who came of the same blood as Uthir, was a potential heir. Let him come and show what he was made of in this war.

"And from the Church," Artor went on, "I will ask only a tithe of grain—"

The abbot of Saint Germanus, who was also bishop for Dumnonia, sat up suddenly.

"It is for men to tithe to the Church, not the Church to men!"

Cups and platters jumped as Artor's fist struck the table, impatience getting the better of him at last, and everyone sat up and paid attention.

"Do you wish your brethren in Gallia to pay in blood instead? The Frankish king may call himself a Christian, but his warriors have little respect for churchmen. The murdered monks win a martyr's crown, but that does little good to the souls for whom they cared!"

In the silence that followed he sensed movement under the

table. He had drawn back his foot to kick, thinking it a dog, when he heard a giggle. Frowning, he pushed back his chair, reached down, and hauled up by the neck of his tunic the small, dark-haired boy who had been hiding there.

"And whose pup are you?" Artor tried to gentle his tone as he set the boy on his knee.

The color that had left the child's face flooded back again. "Marc'h . . . son of Constantine. . . ."

The king shook his head, smiling. "I think you are Cunomorus, a great hunting dog who is waiting to steal the bones! Here's one for you, with the meat still on—" He took a pork rib from his platter, put it in the boy's grubby hand, and set him down. "Run off now and gnaw it!"

Flushing again at the men's laughter, the child scampered away.

"My lord, I am sorry—" Constantine's face was nearly as red as his son's.

"He's a fine lad, and does you credit," answered Artor, with a momentary twinge of regret because he had not known his own son's childhood. "Enjoy him while you can." Perhaps, when his army was assembling at Portus Adurni, he would have the time to visit Medraut in Venta and say farewell.

He looked down the table, his expression sobering, and the Dumnonians sighed and prepared to take up the argument once more. If they fought in battle as hard as they were fighting in council, Artor thought ruefully, this campaign was certain to go well.

Medraut walked with his father along the bank of the Icene, where some forgotten Roman had planted apple trees. Long untended, they had grown tall and twisted; the ground between them littered with branches brought down by storms. But the trees had survived, and on their branches the green apples were beginning to swell.

I am like those apples, thought Medraut. *Wild and untended, still I grow, and no power can keep me from fulfilling my destiny.*

Just over the hill, three thousand men were camped in tents of hide; the meadows behind them were full of horses, but here in the old orchard they might have been in a land deserted since the last legion sailed over the sea. To Medraut, Britannia still held a world of wonders. Why did the king want to go away?

Artor was gazing across the marshes, his eyes clouded by memory.

"I fought a battle here, when I was a little younger than you..." said the king. "The man I loved best in the world was killed, and I took Oesc, who became my friend, as a hostage."

"And now I am hostage to Ceretic's son—" observed Medraut. "How history repeats itself!"

Artor gave him a quick look, and Medraut realized he had not entirely kept the bitterness out of his tone. Since they had last met he had gotten taller, and he no longer had to look up to meet his father's eyes.

"They are not treating you well?" There was an edge to the king's reply that made Medraut smile.

For a moment he considered telling Artor that Cynric had been harsh to him just to see what his father would do. But whether or not Artor believed him, the consequences would not serve his purpose. He shook his head, scooped up a little green apple that had fallen untimely, and began to toss it from hand to hand.

"Oh they have been kind enough. Indeed, they remind me of my own tribesmen in the North. No doubt I fit better here than I would among the cultured magnates of Demetia. That, if anything, is my complaint. I left my mother's dun because I wanted to learn about my father's world."

"Would you rather I sent you to Londinium?" Artor asked, frowning. "I suppose I could arrange for you to be tutored there. Or perhaps one of the monasteries..."

"*Father!*" Medraut did not try to keep the mockery from his laugh. "You cannot imagine that the good monks would welcome *me*! Nor do I wish a tutor! If you want me to learn the ways of the Romans, take me with you to Gallia! You have just told me—at my age, you were fighting battles. Do you want the Saxons to be your son's instructors in the arts of war?"

He watched as anger flushed and faded in the king's face, or was it shame? *He grows uncomfortable when I remind him,* Medraut noted, *but he is too honest to deny it.* It had occurred to him, some months into his exile, that Artor could easily deny their relationship and brand him a deluded child. He realized now that it would be against the king's nature to do that—it was a useful thing to know.

"I wish they did not teach their own!" came the muttered reply. "But you must learn from them what you can. You are getting your growth, but if you were with me there would still be danger. In Gallia the priests have great influence. I will have a hard enough time getting them to accept *me....*"

And your incestuous bastard would be a burden you do not want to bear! It would have been different if his father had loved him. But why should he? Medraut knew well that his begetting had been an accident, and his birth a revenge. He should count himself lucky that the king felt any responsibility towards him at all.

It did not occur to him to wonder why he should want Artor's love. There was only the pain of realization, and an anger he did not even try to understand.

"So you will not take me with you?"

"I cannot—" Artor spread his hands, then let them fall to his side. He turned and began to walk once more. "I am leaving the government of Britannia in the hands of my queen. If there is trouble here, you must go to Guendivar."

Medraut nodded, then, realizing his father could not see him, mumbled something the king could take as agreement. His eyes were stinging, and he told himself it was the wind. But as anguish welled up within him, he threw the apple in his hand with all his strength. It arched up and out, then fell into the river with a splash. Together he and Artor watched as the current caught and carried it towards the sea.

THE HIGH QUEEN

A.D. 507—512

At Camalot someone was always coming or going, and one got used to the noise, especially now, when a series of hot days in early June had opened every window and door. But the voices outside the small building where the queen did her accounts were getting louder. Guendivar set down the tallies of taxes paid in beef or grain as Ninive came in, her fair hair curling wildly in the damp heat.

"My lady—there's a rider, with messages from Gallia—"

The queen's heart drummed in her breast, but she had learned to show no sign. Suddenly she could feel the fine linen of her tunica clinging to back and breast, and perspiration beading on her brow. But she waited with tightly folded hands as the messenger, his tunic still stained with salt from the journey oversea, came in.

"The king is well—" he said quickly, and she realized that her face had betrayed her after all, but that did not matter now. She recognized Artor's seal on the rawhide case in which he sent his dispatches, and held out her hand. The swift, angular writing that she had come to know so well blurred, then resolved into words.

"*. . . and so I am settled once more at Civitas Aquilonia. The*

72

rains have been heavy here, and there is some sickness among the men, but we hope for better weather soon."

She would have been happy to share the sunshine they were having here. But if the weather on both sides of the narrow sea was the same, Armorica would be drying out by now. Artor had not been used to write to her when he travelled in Britannia. But now the queen seemed to be his link to home. Deciphering his handwriting was only one of the many skills she had acquired since the king left her to rule in his name.

"The news from the south of Gallia continues bad, at least for the kingdom of Tolosa. Chlodovechus is moving against the Goths at last, and this time I do not think Alaric will be able to hold. For us, it means peace for as long as it takes for the Franks to digest their new conquest. But in another year or two, they will look about them and notice that this last Roman stronghold is still defying them.

"I judge that I have that long to forge alliances among the British chieftains of Armorica that will withstand the storm. Dare I hope to restore the Empire of the West? I no longer know—but where once I saw Gallia as territory to be regained, now I see men who have put their trust in me, and whom I must not betray. . . ."

There was a break in the writing. The remainder of the letter was written in a different shade of ink, the writing more angular still.

"Tolosa has fallen. The Visigoths are in full retreat, and the Franks boast that they will keep them on the run all the way to the Pyrenaei montes and beyond. They are probably correct. Alaric must want very much to put a range of mountains between him and his foes. He will be safe in Iberia, for a time. But I predict that one day a Frankish king will follow, dreaming of Empire. Unless, that is, we can break their pride. Already we are seeing refugees from Tolosa, both Romans and Goths. If they wish to join the fight here they will be welcome. Some, I may send to you in Britannia.

"Watch well over my own kingdom, my queen. You hold my heart in your hands. . . ."

How, she wondered, was she to take that? Surely, Artor was referring to the land, but for a moment she wondered what it would be like to claim not only his duty, but his love.

She had almost understood it, listening to Merlin's poetry. But even unclothed, Artor kept his spirit armored, and the moment of possibility had passed. It would require some power even greater than Merlin's, she thought sadly, to bring him to her arms. . . .

She tried to tell herself that her husband's absence had at last made her a queen. Was she still fair? She did not know—men had learned that she was better pleased by praises for her wisdom. She had grown into the authority Artor had laid upon her, and discovered that she had a talent for rule. She might have failed him as a wife, but not as Britannia's queen.

But each letter revealed more of the man hidden within the king, the human soul who had guarded himself so carefully when they were alone. Artor had been back to Britannia only three times since beginning the Gallian campaign, brief visits spent settling disputes between the princes or persuading them to send him more men. Guendivar had scarcely seen him.

And she missed him, this husband whom she was only now coming to know. If it was her beauty that had unmanned him, she hoped that she had lost it. She reached for a piece of vellum, and after a moment began to set down words.

"To my lord and husband, greetings. The weather here has turned hot and fair and we have hope for a good harvest. I can send you some of last year's grain store now, and the taxes from Dumnonia. Gualchmai has brought his wife to Camalot. She is an intelligent woman, well read in the Latin poets, not at all the sort one would have expected Gualchmai to choose. But he is happy with her—the wild boy grown up at last. The news from the North is not so good. Morgause writes that your lady mother is ailing. If we hear more, I will send you word. . . ."

Guendivar paused, remembering the lake that lay like a jewel in the lap of the mountains, and the hush that one feared to break with any but sacred sounds. She had been there only once, but the memory was vivid. And yet she had no desire to return. She was a child of the southern lands, and her heart's home was the Vale of Afallon.

* * *

Merlin moved through the forest as a stag moves, scarcely stirring a leaf as he passed. But when he reached the river he was an otter, breasting the surface with undulant ease. When night came, the senses of a wolf carried him onward. But when he noticed at last that he was weary, he sank down between the roots of an ancient oak and became a tree.

Waking with the first light of morning, he thought for a moment that he was a bird. The pain of limbs that had stiffened with inaction brought him back to awareness of his body. He stretched out one forelimb, blinking at the sinewy length of a human arm, furred though it was with wiry, silver-brindled hair. Splayed twigs became fingers that reached out to the smooth, rune-carved wood of the Spear, which he had continued to carry through all his transformations.

With that touch, full consciousness returned to him, and he remembered his humanity. To stay a bird would have been easier, he thought grimly. A bird had no thought beyond the next insect, the next song. The long thoughts of trees, slowly stretching towards the skies, would be better still. A man could remember the message that had started him on this journey; a man could weep, trying to imagine a world without Igierne.

He gazed at the wooded heights above him and knew that the instinct that guided him had led him deep into the Lakeland hills, where once the Brigantes had ruled. A few hours more would bring him to the Isle of Maidens. Animal senses tugged at his awareness—he scented wild onion on the hillside, and grubs beneath a fallen log. Food he must have, and water, but it was necessary that he complete this journey as a man.

When Merlin came to the Lake it was nearing noon. The water lay flat and silver beneath the blue bowl of the sky; even the trees stood sentinel with no leaf stirring. Human reason told him that such calms often preceded storms, but a deeper instinct gibbered that the world was holding its breath, waiting for the Lady of the Lake to give up her own. When he climbed into the coracle drawn up on the shore, he pushed off carefully, as if even the ripples of his passage might be enough to upset that fragile equilibrium.

*   *   *

The priestesses had set Igierne's bed in the garden, beneath a wickerwork shade. Merlin would have thought her dead already if he had not seen the linen cloth that covered her stir. Nine priestesses stood around her, chanting softly. As he approached, the woman who sat at the head of the bed straightened, and he saw that it was Morgause. The clear light that filtered through the wicker showed clearly the lines that had been carved into her face by passion and by pride, but it revealed also the enduring strength of bone. Distracted by the surface differences in coloring and the deeper differences in spirit, he had never realized how much she looked like her mother.

Igierne's eyes were closed; her breathing labored and slow. Her silver hair rayed out upon the pillow, combed by loving hands, but he could see the skull beneath the skin.

"How long—"

"Has she lain thus?" asked Morgause. "She weakened suddenly two days since."

"Have you called on the power of the Cauldron?"

Morgause shook her head, frowning. "She forbade it."

Merlin sighed. He should have expected that, for the power of the Cauldron was to fulfill the way of nature, not to deny it. Morgause spoke again.

"Yesterday she would still take broth, but since last night she has not stirred. She is going away from us, and there is nothing I can do."

"Have *you* slept?" When she shook her head, he touched her hand. "Go, rest, and let me watch awhile. I will call you if there is any change."

It was good advice, though Merlin did not know if he had given it for her sake, or his own. Her anger and her need battered against his hard-won composure.

When she had gone he leaned the Spear against the post, sat down in her place, and took Igierne's hand. It was cool and dry; only when he pressed could he feel the pulse within. He closed his eyes, letting his own breathing deepen, matching his life-force to hers.

"*Igierne . . . my lady . . . Igierne. . . .*" Awareness extended; he felt himself moving out of the body, reaching for that place where her spirit hovered, tethered to her body by a silver cord that thinned with every beat of her heart.

"Merlin, my old friend—" He sensed Igierne as a bright presence, turning towards him. *"Do not tell me I must come back with you, for I will not go!"* The radiance that surrounded them quivered with her laughter.

"Then let me come with you!"

"Your flesh is still bound to the earth. It is not your time. . . ."

"The years pass, yet my body only grows stronger. The only thing that held my spirit to the human world was my love for you!"

"When you wandered, I watched over you from the Lake . . ." came her reply. *"Now I will love you from the Hidden Realm. It is not so far away—"*

He could sense that this was true, for beyond the flicker of her spirit, a bright doorway was growing. He was aware that Morgause had returned, but her grief could not touch him now. From a great distance, it seemed, his mortal senses told him that Igierne's breath came harshly, rattling in her chest. The chanting of the priestesses faltered as someone began to weep, then resumed.

"Your children still need you—" he thought hopelessly.

"My children are grown! Surely they know I love them. Merlin, you would not condemn me to live on in a body that is outworn! Help me, my dear one. Let me go!"

He was not so sure of that, but it was his own need, not that of Morgause, that reached out and drew the spirit of the younger woman into the link as well.

"There you are, my daughter—you see—" Igierne moved closer to the light. *"This is what I tried to tell you. There is only this last bit, that is a little . . . difficult, and then all will be well. This, too, is part of your training. Help me. . . ."*

He could sense when the turmoil in Morgause's spirit began to give way to wonder.

"You see the doorway opening before you—" The words that the younger woman whispered came from ritual, but they carried conviction now, and resonated in both worlds. "The bright spirits of those you love await you, ready to welcome you home. . . ."

And as she spoke, Merlin realized that it was so. He glimpsed those radiant beings drawing nearer, and recognized, with a certainty beyond the senses, Uthir, and behind him Igierne's parents, Amlodius and Argantel.

"Go through the gate. Let our love support you through your own self-judgment. Over you the dark shall have no power. Farewell—we release you into the Lady's waiting arms. . . ."

Somewhere far away, the failing body struggled for breath, sighed, and was still. But that hardly mattered. For a moment, Merlin's inner vision embraced the brightness and he saw Igierne clearly, growing ever younger as she moved away from them until she was the gold-crowned maiden whom he had loved. And then she passed through the portal. The Light intensified beyond mortal comprehension, and Merlin was blown back into the pallid illumination of an earthly day.

The surface of the lake wrinkled as wind brushed the water. A vanguard of cloud was just rising beyond the western hills. Morgause shivered, though the temperature had barely begun to drop; the cold she felt came from the soul. Merlin, beside her, moved as she had seen men move coming half-stunned from the battlefield.

"It was a good death—" she said aloud. "Why am I so angry?" Behind them the ritual wailing of the priestesses swelled and faded like the rising wind, but Morgause felt her throat hard, the muscles tight, and her eyes were dry.

"Because your mother has abandoned you," came the deep rumble of his reply. "Even a death less triumphant than this one is a release for the one who passes. We grieve for ourselves, because she has left us alone."

Morgause stared. For most of her life she had hated this man, the architect of her father's death and her mother's first treachery. Of all people in the world, she had not expected him to understand.

"I remember when my grandmother was dying," she said then. "My mother wept, while I played, uncomprehending, on the shore. Argantel foretold that I would be the Lady of the Lake one day. For so many years I fought my mother, fearing she would deny me my destiny. And now that fate is come upon me, and I am afraid."

"So was she . . ." answered Merlin. "Like you, she had been long away from the Lake. But you have had your mother's teaching. Much of the old wisdom has been lost—it is for you to preserve what you can. I do not know your mysteries . . ." he said with some difficulty, "but you have the Cauldron. Call upon your Goddess—surely She will comfort you."

"And you—" she answered him.

Merlin shook his head. "My goddess has gone out of the world. . . ."

Morgause looked at him in amazement, understanding only now that this man, like her father, had been denied Igierne's love. The wind blew again, more strongly, hissing in the trees. Merlin had turned to gaze across the lake to the heights where, even in those few moments, the clouds had doubled their size.

"I must go—" he said then. "Your mother is High Queen now in the Otherworld, and in this world, the Tiernissa is Guendivar. But you are Lady of the Lake, Morgause—the Hidden Queen, the White Raven of Britannia. Guard it well!"

He held her gaze, and she saw a woman crowned with splendor reflected in his eyes.

"I am the Lady of the Lake . . ." she affirmed, accepting his vision of her at last. "And who are you?"

The certainty in Merlin's eyes flickered out, to be replaced by desolation. "I am a leaf blown by the wind . . . I am a sea-smoothed rock . . . I am a sun-bleached bone . . . I do not know what I am, save that my body lives still in a world that my spirit finds strange. Up there"—he gestured towards the hills—"perhaps I may learn. . . ."

Above the trees, one entered the kingdom of the wind. Merlin struggled upward, reeling as a new gust swept across the slope and the purple bells of the heather rang with soundless urgency. A wren was tossed skyward, crying, caught by the blast. Clouds boiled above him, flinging splatters of rain. Merlin stumbled, jabbed the Spear into the earth to keep his balance, and pulled himself upright once more.

"Blow! Blow! Cry out in rage!" he shouted, shaking his fist at the sky. This violence of nature might be harsh to the body, but it matched the anguish in his soul. "World, weep, let my grief gust forth with every blast of wind!"

He took a step forward, realized he could climb no higher, and sank to his knees. "Why—" he gasped, "am I still alive?"

There were words in the blast that whipped at hair and beard. Merlin grasped the shaft of the Spear, feeling it thrum beneath his hands like a tree in the wind, and abruptly their meaning became clear.

"*Unless you will it, you shall not leave this world. . . .*"

"Am I less than human, then?"

"*Perhaps you are more. . . .*"

Merlin shivered. The Voice was all around him, in the wail of the wind, the vibration of the spearshaft, the rasp of air in his throat. He shook his head.

"Who are you?"

The air rippled with laughter. "*I am every breath you take, every thought you think; I am ecstasy.*" The laughter rolled once more. "*You carry My Spear. . . .*"

Merlin recoiled. "The god of the Saxons!"

"*You may call me that, or Lugos, if it makes you feel easier, or Mercurius. I have walked in many lands, and been called by many names. When men use wit and will and words, I am there. And you have borne my Spear for a dozen winters. Why are you so surprised?*"

"Why did you allow it? What do you want with me?"

"*O, man of Wisdom! Even now, do you not understand?*"

Abruptly the wind failed. The storm was passing. Merlin stared as the light of sunset, blazing suddenly beneath the clouds, filled the world with gold. His grief for Igierne might never leave him, but now his mind buzzed with phrases, riddles, insights and imaginings, and a great curiosity. Holding onto the Spear, he levered himself upright once more. Then he plucked it from the earth and started down the mountain.

Dust rose in golden clouds, stirred by the feet of the harvesters. The cart they drew was piled with sheaves of corn and garlanded with summer flowers. Singing rose in descant to the rhythmic creak of wheels as they pushed it towards the meadow below the villa where the harvest feast had been laid. Guendivar, sitting with Cai and Gualchmai in the place of honor, drew her veil half over her face. But the precaution was needless, for as evening drew nearer, a light breeze had come up to blow the dust away.

She had been glad of Cai's invitation to keep the festival in the place where Artor had been a boy. It was Cai's home now, though the king's service had allowed him to spend little time here. His health had not been good, and she had come partly in hopes of getting him to take some rest. He did seem to be better here. She had smiled at his stories, trying to imagine the great king of Britannia as an eager boy. Her only regret was that Artor was not here with them. Five years he had spent campaigning in Gallia, with little result that she could see. He had not even returned when his mother died the year before.

The procession rounded the last curve, and she heard the chorus more clearly:

"Oh where is he hidden, and where has he gone?
The corn is all cut, and the harvest is done!"

The workers who had cut and bound the last sheaf, that they called "the neck," or sometimes, "the old man," held it high. They had already been soaked with water from the river to bring luck, but in this weather they did not seem to mind. Guendivar remembered with longing the secret pool where she used to bathe when she was a girl, and how she and Julia had discovered the pleasure their bodies could bring. These days, most of the time she felt as virgin as the Mother of God, but as she watched the reapers pursuing the women who had followed to bind the sheaves, she had to suppress a spurt of envy for the fulfillment she had been denied.

"In the first flush of springtime, the young king is born
The ploughed fields rejoice in the growth of the corn—
Oh where is he hidden, and where—"

Guendivar felt unexpected tears prick in her eyes. Men called her the Flower Bride and swore that her beauty was unchanged. But it was not the way of nature for spring to last forever. . . .

The cart was drawn up before the tables and the men who had hitched themselves to it threw off the traces. The woman who had been carrying the last sheaf handed it over to laughing girls, who bore it to the central upright of the drying shed and tied it there, wreathed with flowers. The light of the setting sun, slanting through the trees, turned stalk and seed to gold.

"The sun rises high and the fields they grow green.
Our king now is bearded, so fair to be seen—"

Cai held out his beaker to be refilled as the serving girl came by and sat back with a sigh. "It seems strange to sit here drinking cider, after so many years of war."

"And Artor not here to enjoy it," Gualchmai replied. "It is not right for the king to be so long from his own land. If he had the army with which we won at Mons Badonicus, by now he would be emperor!"

Still singing, men and women joined hands and began to dance around the post.

"The sun rises high and the fields turn to gold,
The king hangs his head, now that he has grown old—"

"Too many died on the quest for the Cauldron, and some of us are getting older . . ." He eyed Gualchmai wryly, rubbing his left arm as if it pained him. "Except, of course, for you."

Gualchmai frowned, uncomprehending. Years of war had battered his face like bronze, the sandy hair was receding from his high brow, but his arms were still oak-hard.

"It is too peaceful," he said truculently, and Guendivar laughed. "My lord set me here to guard you, but all our enemies are still frightened of his name." He sighed, and then turned to look at her, his eyes pleading. "Let me go to him, lady. Those Frankish lords would not dare to laugh if I were with him. Artor needs me. I am of use to no one here!"

"The reaper swings high and the binder bends low,
The king is cut down and to earth he must go."

Guendivar shivered, touched by a fear she thought she had forgotten. For so long, Artor had been a bodiless intelligence that spoke to her through the written word, she had nearly forgotten he wore mortal flesh that was vulnerable to cold, hunger, and enemy swords.

"Ninive, bring me my shawl—" she said, but the girl was not there. It should not have surprised her; the child made no secret of her discomfort in large gatherings. No doubt she was wandering in the woods on the hill, and would return when darkness fell. And in truth, the chill the queen felt was an internal one, that neither shawl nor mantle could ease.

"Very well—" Both men turned to look at her. "It comforts me to have you here, and your wife will not thank me for letting you go, but I agree that Artor needs you more."

The harvesters rushed inward towards the last sheaf, arms upraised.

"And we shall make merry with bread and with beer,
Until he returns with the spring of the year. . . ."

Then the circle dissolved into laughter as they descended on the vats of harvest ale.

Grinning, Gualchmai downed his own in a single swallow and held out his cup for more.

"But be sure that you make good on your boast, my champion," Guendivar said then. "Beat the breeches off the Franks and bring my lord swiftly home."

"Oh where is he hidden, and where has he gone?
The corn is all cut, and the harvest is done!"

Merlin walked in the oakwood above the villa in the golden light of a harvest moon. He had to remind himself that Turpilius and Flavia were both dead these twenty years and the farm belonged to Cai, for seen from the hillside, nothing seemed to have changed. Even from here the sound of celebration came clearly. Around the threshing sheds torches glittered; the revellers moving among them in a flickering dance of light and shadow. Stubbled fields gleamed faintly beyond them, waiting to rest through the fallow moons of wintertide.

He had intended to join the celebration, but the rites of the seeded earth were not his mysteries. Long experience had taught him that his presence would cast a chill on the festival, like a breath of wind from the wilderness beyond their fenced fields. It was far too beautiful a night to sleep, and these days he needed little rest, and had no need for the shelter of walls.

And so he walked, hair stirred lightly by the breathing darkness, feeding on the rich, organic scents of leaf mold and drying hay. On such a night it was easy to forget the dutiful impulse that had sent him south to offer his counsel to Artor's queen. He belonged in the wilderness, with only his daimon for companion and the god of the Spear for guide.

These days, the god was always with him. But the bright spirit that he called his daimon, the companion of his childhood, he had not seen for many years. Now that he was ancient he found himself remembering her bright eyes and shining hair ever more vividly. It was the fate of the old, he had heard, to become childlike.

Thinking so, he laughed softly, and out of the night, like a shiver of bells, came an answer.

Merlin stood still, senses questing outward. It was beyond belief that a man could have been present without his knowledge on this hill. What he found at last was a glimmering whiteness perched in an oak tree, the human mind so tuned to the rhythms of the night he had thought it a perturbation of the wind.

"The hour grows late—" came a silvery voice from the branches. "Why does the greatest Druid in Britannia wander the hills?"

Merlin shaped his sight to an owl's vision and saw a fine-boned face haloed by fair hair. For a moment he could not breathe. It was the face of his daimon, and yet she was no part of his imagining—even as a child, he had always understood the difference between the images that came from outside and those that lived within. And now he could sense the warmth of a human body and hear the faint whisper of breath. She stirred, and he glimpsed the glint of embroidery on her gown.

"Why is a maiden of the court sitting in a tree?"

"You do not know me, and yet we are kin." She laughed again. "I am Gualchmai's daughter by a woman of the hills, and if I cannot be roaming there, in this oak I can at least pretend to be free."

"That is so. I have myself lived for a time in a tree. Would it displease you to have an old man's company?" To his sight, a radiance seemed to flow from her slim form, more lovely than the light of the moon.

She cocked her head like a bird. "I have never before met anyone who felt like a part of the forest. You know all its secrets, is it not so? Stay then, and talk to me. . . ."

Merlin swayed, as if something were melting within him that had been frozen since Igierne died. He put out his hand to the oak tree, and carefully eased himself to the solid ground.

"Gladly . . ." he said softly. "Gladly will I stay with you."

Merlin's return was a wonder that had men buzzing for a season. When they saw how often he walked with the girl Ninive, they laughed, thinking they knew the reason. But Guendivar, having promised Gualchmai that she would watch over his child, understood that there was nothing sexual in the attraction between the old man and the maiden. And she had other, more pressing, concerns.

Gualchmai's departure had not loosed all Britannia's old enemies upon them, as some had feared. The Picts were holding to Artor's treaty, and there was only an occasional raider from Eriu. It was the princes of Britannia who were beginning to grow restive, like horses kept too long in pasture who forget the governance of bit and rein. Merlin told her that after Uthir died it had been the same. The counsel of the Druid was valuable; with his guidance Guendivar grew into her queenship like a tree in fertile soil. But he could not show an iron fist to the princes. She wrote to Artor, but another year passed, and he did not return.

Gualchmai had been gone for two years when new trouble between the men of Dumnonia and the West Saxons impelled her to appeal to Artor again. She had summoned Constantine and Cynric to meet with her at Durnovaria. The spring had been a fine one, and they had no excuse for not traveling. But if she could not reconcile them with her wisdom, she and they both knew that she had no teeth with which to compel obedience.

Through her window came the rich, organic scent of the river that Durnovaria guarded, mixed with the sharper tang of the sea. Few men lived permanently in the town—even the prince preferred to spend most of his time at his villa in the hills. But folk still gathered here for the weekly market, and the clamor of mixed tongues made a deeper background to the crying of gulls. Guendivar set down the vellum on which she had been working and took up the most recent letter that Artor had sent to her.

"Pompeius Regalis paid me a visit last month; he is building a stronghold near Brioc's monastery in the west of the coastal plain and has realized he needs allies. There are so many Dumnonians there now the place is called by their name. His son Fracanus was with him. He has invented a new sport that he persuaded some of my men to try. Instead of racing their horses with chariots, they measure out a course and put up the lightest boys into the saddle. Of course it is dangerous if the lad is thrown, but the horses do go faster. . . ."

Guendivar shook her head. In conversation, Artor had never been one for humor, but in these letters he seemed anxious to amuse as well as to inform her. Indeed, she had learned more of his mind since he went over the sea than when they lived together.

"Summer is almost upon us. I believe that I can get Regalis and Conan of Venetorum to agree to an alliance, and with them, Guenomarcus of Plebs Legionorum. With them behind me, I will count Armorica as secured. The sons of Chlodovechus, having settled mat-

ters in Tolosa, are gazing northward, and the Britons who took up
land in Lugdunensis have asked our aid."

That meant that Artor would be fighting soon, might be in
battle even now. Guendivar realized that her grip had creased
the vellum, and gently let it fall. The king had spent his life
in warfare and rarely taken any harm. And now he had
Gualchmai. Why should the prospect concern her now? Was
it because he was not fighting for Britannia?

From the direction of the city gate came a blare of cow-
horns; the babble in the marketplace crested to a roar. Cynric
had arrived at last. Guendivar closed her eyes, massaging the
skin above her brows. Then she rolled and tied Artor's letter,
stood and called for her maidens to attire her in the stiff cer-
emonial garments of the high queen.

Robed in a Druid's snowy white and leaning on Woden's
Spear, Merlin waited behind the high queen's throne. In almost three years, he had become accustomed to wearing civ-
ilized garments once more. Ninive accepted the weight of
woven cloth and metal pins when she wanted to run like a
wild pony across the moors. For her sake, he could do the
same.

Men wondered what deep purpose lay behind his return,
but he had no plan, no intentions. In his heart he knew that
Ninive was not his daimon incarnate in a maiden's flesh. But
she held him to the human world. He looked at her now,
standing with the other girls who served the queen. For a
moment their eyes met, and he heard the cry of a falcon soaring above the headlands, and the hushed roar of the sea.

The long chamber where once the magistrates of Durnovaria had held their meetings was beginning to fill. Constantine sat on the south side with the chieftain whose lands lay
on the Saxon border beside him. A half dozen of his houseguard muttered behind him, fists straying to their hips and
then away when they remembered that they had been required to leave their swords outside.

A side door opened and he saw Guendivar, framed like an
icon against the darkness of the passageway. She was man-
tled in gold, her pointed face framed by the pearl lappets of

a Byzantine diadem. But the splendor in which she walked was only a visible focus for the penumbra of power, and men rose to greet her with a reverence that was more than formal. The queen ascended the dais and took her seat, and the two youths who had escorted her, one red as a fox, the other fair, took their places to either side of the carved chair. Eormenric looked about him smiling, but red Ceawlin gazed at the door with a face like carved bone.

The double doors at the end of the hall swung open. Tall men came through it. The flaming hair of their leader was dusted now with ash, but it was bright enough to set an answering flame ablaze in Ceawlin's eyes.

"*Waes hael, drighten. Wilcume!*" said the queen, who had learned a little Saxon from her hostages.

Cynric blinked, then brought up his arm in acknowledgment. He and his men wheeled and took their places on the northern wall.

Merlin let his mind drift, the point and counterpoint of complaint and accusation like the mutter of distant thunder. Behind Cynric he could just make out a darker head amongst the fair and brown. The Saxon leader stepped forward, gesturing, and a ray of light from the upper window touched the head of the man behind him with a gleam of bronze. That was no Saxon! Merlin stepped out from behind the queen's chair, extending other, secret, senses towards the stranger.

As if he had felt the touch, the bronze-haired man straightened and turned, and Merlin recoiled, recognizing, in a face that was a masculine reflection of Morgause, the grey gaze of Artor the king. Any other identity of form or feature might have been put down to their common inheritance from Igierne, but not those eyes, which had come to Artor from Uthir, who was father to him alone.

"Lady, as you have deemed, so shall it be. Eadwulf will bring his kinsmen back from the western bank of the river. We give up our claim to the land—" Cynric's voice grew louder, and the Dumnonian lords began to grin. "I call your *Witan*, your council, to witness that we of the West Seax have kept faith with you. In your hall my son has grown to manhood. You have taught him much. Now it is time for him to come back to his own land and learn the ways of the folk that he will one day rule. In exchange, I return to you the son of your king!"

As Medraut stepped forward, a whisper of amazement, of question, of commentary swept the hall like the wind that heralds the storm. Those who remembered the Pendragon were marking the resemblance that identified Medraut not only as Artor's nephew but as his son. The tablet-woven banding on his dark tunic was all Saxon, like the seax-knife that hung at his side. But the brooch that held his mantle was of Pictish work, and the pride of the House of Maximian shone in his eyes. He halted, and half a hundred glances flickered from his face to that of the queen.

Surely, thought Merlin, Artor must have told her—but for nine years Medraut had been hidden among the Saxons like a hound among wolves. It had been too easy for all of them to forget that one day he would return to hunt with his own pack once more.

If she was surprised, Guendivar gave no sign. Speaking softly, she turned to Ceawlin, and the eagerness burning in his eyes for a moment dimmed as he bent to kiss her hand.

"I will not forget you, lady," he said hoarsely. Then, as if she had slipped his leash, he bounded to his father's side.

"And Eormenric"—she turned to the other youth—"you have spent as many years among us as your father did when he was young. I will not keep you here when your companion has gone."

For a moment the fair lad's face flamed. "My father loved King Artor," he said in a low mice. "But my loyalty is given to *you*. If ever you have need of me, you have only to call." He bent his head, turned, and went out of the hall.

Cynric and his son had moved a little aside, so that Medraut stood alone. Would the queen welcome him? Would she spurn him? Would she hail him as nephew or son? His face had gone very white, and as he looked at Guendivar, something anguished flickered in his eyes.

Fragmented images fluttered behind Merlin's vision. He grasped for them, and for a moment glimpsed dark shapes battling beneath the hard light of noon. His spirit reached out for comprehension to the daimon who from childhood had guided him, and in the next moment he found he was staring at Ninive, standing solid and alive beside the queen. For so long he had fled the power of foreknowledge that had haunted his childhood. Now, when he needed it, the only meaning he understood lay in the fair face of one young girl.

Guendivar leaned forward, stretching out her hand. "Come, Medraut—I bid you welcome home. . . ."

VI

A WIND FROM THE NORTH

A·D· 513

"MY LADY, A MAN HAS COME—FROM GALLIA. . . ."
Medraut's voice was quiet, the northern burr worn smooth
by his years among the Saxons. Guendivar dropped the ball
of embroidery wool she had been winding. As it rolled across
the floor, Medraut bent smoothly and scooped it up, handing
it back to her with a bow. Since he had been so unexpectedly
returned to them, he had become an accepted presence in her
court.

The thin lad who had appeared so briefly at Camalot nine
years before had never met her eyes. Now she understood
why, knowing him for Artor's son. She was glad that the king
had told her himself, and not left her to learn it from gossip,
or worse still, from Cynric. If Medraut's birth troubled him,
he no longer let it show. His mother had trained him well,
the queen thought wryly—he certainly knew how to make
himself useful among the women. But his silent appearances
still startled her, and she was no closer to understanding him.

"With news?" It was three months since she had heard
from Artor, and a wet winter was turning into a chilly spring.

"He bears letters, but he is no messenger—"

At the sardonic tone, Guendivar lifted one eyebrow, but to

comment would be to admit weakness, and instinct and experience both told her that with this one she must always seem strong.

"Shall I receive him here, or make him wait for a formal audience?" she asked, waiting curiously for his reply.

Since Medraut's arrival, she had searched her soul, grateful that she had suppressed her first furious impulse to send the boy back to Morgause. He had not asked to be born. Certainly, she thought with some resentment, she could not conceive when the king was in Gallia, even if Artor had been potent in her bed. Medraut was Artor's only son; even with his ambiguous heritage, he could be Artor's heir.

"Not here—" Medraut gazed around at the domestic clutter of the Women's Sunhouse. "And yet, I think this man is one you will wish to bind to your service. His name is Theodoric, a Goth of the kingdom of Tolosa and a man of the sea. Dress richly, but meet him in the garden."

Guendivar nodded slowly. Whether or not Medraut had the instinct for kingship, he certainly understood how to manipulate men. She glanced at the angle of the sun.

"That is good advice. Just after noon, bring him to me there."

Guendivar was already waiting on the stone bench beside the lavender bush when Theodoric entered the garden. One forgot that for a hundred years the Goths had been part of the Empire, not always peacefully, to be sure, but living side by side with Romans, learning their ways and their laws. They were even some kind of heretical Christians, she had heard. Certainly this man, tall and weathered by sun and wind though he might be, was no barbarian.

"I am Theodoric son of Theudebald—" The Goth stopped before her, bowing.

The queen rose to meet him, extending her hand. "Praefectus Classis," she continued in Latin, "be welcome to Britannia. Has my husband given you letters to bring to me?"

"He has, and said that to deliver them safely should be my best recommendation to you. I parted from the lord Artor on the last day of February." From the case at his side he drew a tubular letter case and held it out to her.

"Truly?" she said, calculating, "then you have made a swift passage. In a moment I will read what he has to say of you, but for now you must tell me about yourself, and why you have come."

"Lady, I need a home." A flush stained the bronzed cheeks, but he met her eyes steadily. "The Franks have driven my people over the mountains and into Iberia. The Goths are carving out a new kingdom, but it is all inland, whereas I am a man of the sea. I know how to sail it, how to fight upon it, how to build ships and defend harbors."

"And Britannia has many miles of coastline, and enemies who attack her from the sea—" finished Guendivar. "Now I understand why Artor sent you."

He straightened, relieved, but not surprised at her understanding. *What*, she wondered, *did Artor tell him about me?*

"What remains of the Gothic navy waits at Aquilonia—five vessels with their crews and captains who will sail at my command. I offer it to you."

"Our most present danger is the Irish, who attack the coasts of Demetia at will. Make your base at Glevum—I will send to the lord Agricola, who rules Demetia, to provide you with supplies. With your skills and his resources, we may hope to dislodge the Irish who have settled there and discourage them from trying again. Does that sound well to you?"

"It does indeed," he breathed. "I will write to my men immediately, and my ship can carry any messages you may have for the lord Artor." He started to turn, then paused, staring at her. "But perhaps you will want to read the king's letter first. To take me at my own word like this—you are very trusting."

"Perhaps." She smiled. "Although, if I have second thoughts, I can always send riders after you. But I hope that my lord would not have left his land in my charge if he did not trust my ability to read men."

For a moment longer Theodoric looked at her. Then, once again he bowed, not the courteous inclination with which he had greeted her, but the full reverence he might have made at the court of an emperor.

"Domina, I came here hoping to find safe harbor. But I have also found a queen. . . ."

Guendivar felt her own cheeks growing warm, but managed a gracious nod. "Medraut—" she called. She had not seen him, but she suspected he would not be out of earshot, and indeed it was only a moment before he appeared. "Escort our new admiral and help him to whatever he needs."

When he had gone, she sat down on the bench once more, and with fingers that trembled a little, opened the leather tube and pulled out the vellum roll inside.

"*My lady, I must write swiftly, for Theodoric wishes to catch the morning tide. He has a good reputation among the Goths, and seems a sensible man, but we here have no need for a navy. I give him to you for the defense of Demetia. Use him well.*

"*The Franks have marched more swiftly than I expected, despite the rain, and our supplies are getting low. Whatever you can send will be very welcome. The sons of Chlodovechus quarrel among themselves, but they can combine efficiently enough when they recognize an enemy. So far Theuderich, the eldest and most experienced among them, is still holding onto the leadership, even though he is not the son of Queen Chlotild, but of a concubine.*

"*Yesterday they brought us to battle, a hard-fought, muddy encounter that left no clear victor. We did not retreat—perhaps that may be counted as a victory. But it was costly. My nephew Aggarban was killed in the fighting, and there are many wounded.*

"*Riothamus still lives, but he is failing. Soon, I fear he will leave us, and I will have to decide whether or not to claim his sovereignty. I care for these people, and I believe that many of them have come to look to me with love and loyalty. But this is not my land. Last summer my journeys took me deep into Gallia, and there I found a town called Aballo, which in our tongue is the same as Afallon, the place of apples. And I closed my eyes, and saw the vale and the Tor so clearly I nearly wept with longing to be there. And you were there, standing beneath the apple trees.*"

There was a break in the writing there, as if he had been distracted, or perhaps too overcome to continue. Guendivar found her own eyes prickling with unshed tears, and shook her head. *How can you write such things,* she wondered angrily, *and not come home to me?* Wiping her eyes, she picked up the scroll once more.

"You will have to tell Medraut about his brother's death. About the boy himself, I do not know what to say. I did not understand him that season he was with me, and I cannot imagine what nine years among the Saxons have made of him. I can only trust that the powers that protect Britannia had some purpose in bringing him to birth."

Once more there was a space. The writing that followed was smaller, and precise, as if he had been exerting all his control.

"You, my queen, are the one most wronged by his existence. If you, of your charity, will keep him by you I will be grateful, but if it seems better, send him away. I leave him in your hands."

There was a blot on the page, as if he had started to write *"I wish . . ."* and then crossed it out. Beyond that she saw only the scrawled letters of his name.

"I wish!" Guendivar repeated aloud, glaring at the page and wondering whether this was trust or desperation. Should she be honored or angry? Either way, Medraut was her problem now. She would have to make another attempt to talk to him.

Artor, Artor, you have been too long away. What will it take to bring you home again? She rolled up the vellum and slid it into its case once more.

Guendivar had intended to talk with Medraut that evening, but just as they sat down to their meal a messenger arrived. He was from King Icel, his news an attack on Anglia by raiders from the northern land that is called Lochlann in Eriu, and by the Romans Skandza. They had picked their way through the shoals of the Metaris estuary and struck southward through the fens, burning farmsteads and carrying off livestock, goods, and men. Icel did not precisely ask for aid— he had, after all, been given those lands on the understanding that he would defend them—but the implication that he would welcome some support was clear.

"Otherwise, he would have simply reported his victory,"

said Cai. "We must send a troop—enough men so they will know we have not abandoned them. I can raise some from my own country, and perhaps the Dumnonians—"

"Will send no men to aid Saxons, as you know very well!" Guendivar interrupted him. "And you are not going to lead them, whoever they are. I need you here!"

That was not entirely true, but Cai must know as well as she did that he was in no condition for campaigning. He did not protest her decision, and that worried her. In the past year he had grown short of breath, and his high color was not a mark of health. Cai refused to discuss his condition with her or with Merlin. To keep him from exhausting himself further was the most she could manage.

"The messenger will need a day or two to recover. I will think on what we may do."

The queen was still worrying over the problem that evening when Medraut knocked at the door of the accounting house.

For the first time, she regretted allowing Gualchmai to go to Gallia. Or Theodoric to depart for Demetia—but the Anglians would not have been impressed by a Goth newly come to Britannia, no matter how good his navy. And she dared not send a Dumnonian prince, who was as likely to encourage the Northmen to attack Icel as to defend him. She needed someone of unquestioned British background who could deal with the Saxons.

"They are saying," said Medraut as he entered, "that my brother Aggarban is dead."

Guendivar set down the tax rolls she had been pretending to examine. "It is so. He died from wounds taken in battle. I am sorry."

Medraut shrugged. "He was some years older, and left home when I was only five years old. I did not know him well."

There was an uncomfortable silence.

"Will you sit?" she asked finally, setting the scroll she had been pretending to read aside. "The nights are still chilly. I will ask Fulvia to bring us some chamomile tea."

"Let me call her—" There was a hint of indulgence in Medraut's smile. He indicated the table covered with scrolls and wax tablets. "You have labored enough this evening already." He rose and went to the door.

Guendivar kept her face still. In the past six years she had learned to recognize the subtle tension of manipulation. It was unusual to find such skill in a man so young, but she thought that constant practice had made her even more skillful at it than he.

"The Goth, Theodoric, brought letters from the king," she said when Medraut had taken his seat once more.

"—my father," he completed her sentence.

Guendivar lifted an eyebrow. Was that the way he wanted it? "The king your father has left it to me to decide whether to keep you here or to send you elsewhere." She watched Medraut carefully, uncertain whether the tightening she thought she saw in his face came from the flicker of the lamp-flame or from unease.

But if she had worried him, he covered it quickly—when he lifted his head she saw the skin stretched across the strong, graceful bones of his face as smoothly as a mask.

"Since he has abandoned both kith and kingdom, it is fitting that his son, like Britannia, should be in the keeping of his queen. . . ."

"Say, rather, that he has left both in a mother's care . . ." she corrected blandly.

"Oh, pray do not!" Medraut's tone was sardonic, but she could see that she had shaken him. "You forget—my mother is Morgause!"

Guendivar blinked. She was only too aware how Morgause had damaged Artor—for the first time it occurred to her to wonder how she might have warped her son. She thought, *I will be the good mother Medraut never had*, and suppressed the anguished resentment that Artor had never allowed her to be the wife she should have been.

Medraut was still watching her, and Guendivar gave him a gentle smile. "Has your mother turned you against all women, then?"

He shook his head, lamplight sending ripples of flame

along the smooth waves of auburn hair. The grey gaze that was so like Artor's held her own. But as she met his eyes, she realized that the expression there was nothing like Artor's at all.

"And has my father turned you against all men, leaving you to lie in an empty bed for so many years?"

Guendivar stiffened. Medraut's voice was very soft, his eyes hidden now by the sweep of downturned lashes so that she could not tell whether sympathy or irony glimmered there.

"That is not a question you may ask of me!"

"Then who can?" He straightened, and now it was she who could not look away. "Who has a better right to question what happens in King Artor's bed than you and I? We have a unique relationship," he said bitterly. "It was you, my lady, who chose to begin this conversation—you cannot take refuge in the ordinary courtesies now!"

Guendivar struggled to keep her composure. "It is clear," she said tightly, "that you do not want another mother."

"A mother?" He shuddered. "For that, you would have had to take me when I was born. But you were only six years old. Did you realize, my lady, how nearly of an age we are?" He reached out to her.

"What do you want, Medraut? What am I to do with you?" she said desperately, trying to forget that for a moment she had wanted to take his hand.

"Use me! Let me show what I can do, not as Artor's mistake or the tool of Morgause, but as myself, a prince of the line of Maximian!" he exclaimed. "Send me to the Anglians! Who else do you have who can understand them? They will not care about my birth, except to recognize that it is royal. There are stories of such matings in their own lore. With thirty men, or sixty, well-mounted, I could show them that the arm of Britannia is still long, even when her king is away!"

Guendivar could not fault his reasoning. But even as she agreed, she realized that it was not for his sake that she wanted him away, but for her own.

*   *   *

Medraut coughed as a shift in the wind brought the acrid reek of burning thatch. The black horse tossed its head uneasily and he jerked on the rein. The British had joined forces with Icel's men at Camulodunum and followed the trail of burnt farmsteads northward. And now, it would appear they had found the enemy. That same wind carried a singsong gabble of northern voices. He lifted his hand, a swift glance catching the attention of the British who rode behind him and the Anglian spearmen who marched with Creoda, a broad-built young man with ashy brown hair who was Icel's youngest son.

Creoda was the only one of Icel's children born in Britannia. He had been a boy during Artor's Anglian wars, brought up on his elder brother's tales of vanished glories. Medraut had not found it difficult to get him talking—he was much like the sons of the chieftains in Cynric's hall, enjoying the benefits of peace, but chafing because they had been born too late to be heroes. It was only when fending off marauders like these Northmen that they got the chance to fight at all.

Carefully they moved forward, the British on the road, the Anglians spreading out through the tangle of second-growth woodland where the old Roman fields were going back to the wild. Then the road curved, and suddenly the trees were gone. Beyond the young barley that the Anglian settler had planted in his home field they could see the burning farmstead.

Medraut yelled and bent forward, digging his heels into the black's sides. As the horse lurched into a gallop, he dropped the knotted reins on its neck, shrugged his shield onto his arm and plucked his spear from its rest at his side. He noted the bodies of the farmfolk without emotion, attention fixed on the foe. The raiders were dropping their booty and snatching up the weapons they had laid aside, but he had caught them by surprise. They were still scattered when the British hit them, stabbing and slashing with spear and sword.

The buildings were still smouldering when the fighting ended. Medraut drew a deep breath, grinning, exulting in the rush of blood through his veins. It had been like this when he had ridden with Cynric to break up a fight between two feuding clans of Saxons—the tension before the conflict and the exaltation after, as if he were drunk on a dark mead of war. Growing up in the hulking shadows of his brothers, he had sometimes despaired of ever becoming a warrior—but Cynric had trained him well. Though he did not have Goriat's height or Aggarban's heavy muscles, he had learned to make full use of the swift flexibility of his lean frame.

A dozen northern bodies sprawled in the farmyard, blood and mud darkening their fair hair. The rest, near forty in number, stood together by the well, their weapons heaped before them, glaring at the circle of Anglian spearmen who had caught those who tried to flee. Two of Creoda's men had been killed and several wounded; one of the British had broken a leg when he was pulled from his horse. But Medraut himself had not a mark on him, while three of the fallen had died at his hand. He was *good* at fighting—a gift he owed neither to father nor mother, but to Cynric's teaching and his own hard-won skill.

He grinned savagely, surveying his prisoners.

"Does one of you have the Roman tongue?" he asked.

A young man with hair so pale it seemed white in the spring sunlight straightened. Medraut had already guessed him to be the leader from the gold armring he wore.

"*Appeto Galliam—*" he said in rough Latin, using a verb which could mean either traveling to a place or attacking it, to indicate that he had been to Gallia.

"That I can believe!" murmured one of the British.

"*Mercator—*" the Northman continued. *As a merchant—*

"And that, I do not believe at all!"

"*Gippus, filius Gauthagastus regulus.*" The prisoner touched his chest. *Gipp son of Gauthagast. . . .*

"*Medrautus filius Artorius.*" He tapped his own breast, ignoring the little murmur of reaction from his men. "So, we have a king's son to ransom," he added in the Saxon tongue.

"A second son only," said Gipp in the same language. "You will not get much for me."

"Oh, I will get something—" Medraut smiled sweetly. "Where are the others?"

"The rest of you swine!" snarled Creoda when the prisoner did not answer.

"Gone by now, full-laden—" The Northman grinned. "They left us six days ago, but we were still hungry."

"This time, you have bit off more than you can chew," said Creoda, but the news had clearly relieved him.

Medraut nodded. "Who are your best seamen? They shall take your ship back to the North with word to your people. The rest of you will come with us to Camulodunum. Creoda, will you set up a rotation of guards?"

"Gladly! And send a messenger to my father." He favored Medraut with an approving smile. "You fight like one of our own, son of the Bear. We have done good work today!"

The Britons and their Anglian allies moved slowly southward, for some of the Northmen were wounded and could not go fast. But the weather had cleared and the roads were beginning to dry. With all their enemies accounted for, they could afford to relax.

On the third evening, knowing that the next day's march would bring them to Camulodunum, Medraut took a skin of ale and sat down beside his prisoner.

"Tomorrow we will come to Camulodunum," he said, offering the ale.

"A Roman town—who now lives there?" Gipp answered in the same tone. If he harbored fears for his future, he was doing well at hiding them.

"Anglians. The town was falling into ruin. Icel sent one of his chieftains to hold the place by the terms of his treaty with King Artor."

Gipp lifted an eyebrow. "I thought the Anglians conquered this land." He drank, and passed the skin of ale back again.

"Then why do I ride with them?" asked Medraut. "Artor defeated Icel's army twenty years ago. But by then, all the Britons had fled and there was no one to till the land. So Artor took the Anglians into his kingdom, to protect it from raiders."

"Like me. . . ." Gipp grinned. "They do not do so well, eh?"

"They have mostly settled the richer lands inland, not the coasts. Is this land much like your own?"

Gipp laughed. "It would be hard for a place to be more different. Halogaland is all mountains, with little pockets of pasture clinging above the narrow fjords. This land—so flat—" He gestured at the mixed marsh and woodland around them. "Seems very strange. But there are no rocks. A man could grow anything in this soil."

"Have you seen many lands?" Medraut wiped his mouth and passed the ale-skin back again.

"Oh, there are always kings who look for good fighting men. I marched with Ela when he attacked the Geats, after they took in the banished sons of his brother. He killed Heardred, the Geatish king, but Adgils and Admund escaped him. They say Beowulf rules there now, and he is a hero of whom there are already many tales. I think there would be little profit in following Ela now."

"It is profit you look for, not glory?" Medraut rested his forearms on his knees, considering the other man.

Gipp's high-boned face creased in a smile. "They say in my country that cattle and kinsmen will die, and only a man's fame live after. But I have won my name in battle, and it seems to me that so long as I live in this world I will need the cattle and the kin. I would not be sorry to settle down with a plump wife and a good farm. But at home there is little land."

"And that is why you think your father will not ransom you?

Gipp shrugged. "A man cannot escape his wyrd."

"Well—" Medraut got to his feet, motioning to the Northman to keep the ale-skin. "Perhaps we will find some other use for you."

The bright, hot weather of June was smiling on the land when Medraut came back to Camalot. The fortress was full of men and horses—Guendivar had called the princes of Britannia to council, and their retinues sat drinking and dicing in stable and ramparts and hall.

He had stayed with the Anglians long enough to get Icel's agreement to settle Gipp at the mouth of the Arwe, north of Camulodunum, to hold the place for the Anglians as they held the whole of Anglia for Artor. But the Northman knew whom he had to thank for his good fortune. Medraut had not decided what use he might make of the warrior, but it never hurt to have the gratitude of a good fighting man.

Medraut was twenty-six years old. At his age, his father had already been king for ten years. He himself had spent the equivalent years with Cynric, and what had they gotten him?

The sons of the Saxons are not the only ones who dream of glory, he thought ruefully as he gazed at the grizzled locks of the princes who sat at council in the great roundhouse with their sons behind them. *Where, in this empire Artor is building, is there a place for me?*

The queen had summoned the assembly to set the levies for this year's taxes. It was not going well.

"Ten years! Next year it will be ten years since the king was sailing oversea!" exclaimed Cunobelinus, his northern accent striking with a painful familiarity in Medraut's ear. " 'Tis as long, surely, as it took the Greeks to take the city of Troy!"

"And will that be the end of it? Or will Artor, like Ulysses, be another ten years returning home?" Peretur echoed him.

"The seas that separate our shores from Gallia are neither so great nor so treacherous as the Mare Internum," the queen said tartly, "but even if it were so, when Artor returns he will find me as faithful as Penelope."

"My lady—no one doubts your fidelity," Eldaul of Glevum said gently, "only the need for it. The king of Britannia belongs at home."

"Oh, he may bide abroad for another ten years with my good will and conquer all the way to the gates of Roma," put in Paulinus of Viroconium, "so long as he does not require my taxes! Let the men of Gallia support his army if they desire his presence so greatly."

There was a murmur of agreement from many of the others.

"We have done well enough without him, these past

years!" said someone at the other end of the hall. Medraut peered through the shadows and recognized the prince of Guenet.

Cunobelinus turned towards him, glaring. "But without the king, how long will the Pax Artoria be lasting? Drest Gurthinmoch has honored his treaty, but a new generation of warriors is growing up on tales of the riches of Britannia. How long will he be able to hold them? If he thinks that Artor has abandoned us, how long will he try?"

"The king has not abandoned us!" exclaimed Guendivar, two spots of color burning in her cheeks.

Perhaps not, my lady, thought Medraut, *but he certainly appears to have abandoned you!* She was very beautiful in her anger. He thought with distaste of his mother, who had also had to rule alone when Leodonus began to fail. But Morgause had lusted after power.

What do you lust for, Guendivar, he wondered, gazing at her, *or do you even know?* Last night he had dreamed of Kea, the Pictish slave who had been his first woman. Like the queen, she had been sweetly rounded, with hair like amber in the sun. At the time, he had thought her beautiful, but compared to Guendivar's radiance, her light was only an oil-lamp's flame.

"Artor asks for our taxes—for gold and for grain—" Peretur of Eburacum was speaking now. "And for the defense of Britannia we have never denied him—" His grim gaze swept the assembly, as if tallying those who *had* sometimes refused their support, even during the Saxon wars. "But I am loathe to give up resources which, if the Picts break the Border, we will need ourselves!"

The babble of response was like the roar of a distant sea. Guendivar surveyed the assembly, cheeks flaming with anger, and rose to her feet, staring them down until silence fell once more. But when she spoke, her voice was calm.

"Clearly, there are many factors here to be considered, and we have sat long at our debate. Hunger is not the best counselor. Let us go out to the meal that my cooks have been preparing, and meet again when the sun begins its descent once more."

As he followed the others from the roundhouse, Medraut continued to watch the queen. Though her women had come out to escort her, she seemed very much alone, her brow furrowed with the anxiety she had been too proud to show in the hall.

Britannia may be able to endure without Artor, he thought then, *but if he does not return, what will happen to the queen?* His gaze followed her as she entered her own quarters, and he blinked, his vision for a moment overlaid with memory of the dream in which little Kea had lain in his arms.

"Medraut!"

At the shout, he turned, and saw the heir to Viroconium hurrying towards him. Martinus was a puppy, with an open face and eager eyes, but he might have his uses. Medraut paused, arranging his features in a pleasant expression.

"I hear that you fought wild savages from Lochlann last spring. What were they like? How many did you kill?"

With some effort, Medraut maintained his smile. Martinus' voice was both penetrating and loud; others were turning, younger men for the most part, second sons and chieftains' heirs. He saw Caninus of Glevum, who was a good fighter already, and the two cousins from Guenet, Cunoglassus and Maglocun. In another moment, a group was gathering, and Medraut grinned.

"They are fierce fighters indeed, but no monsters. If you like, I will tell you the tale. . . ."

Whatever he might say was bound to be more interesting than the political debates of their elders, thought Medraut as he led his audience to the shade below the palisade.

"You all know that we defeated the Anglians twenty years ago, and gave them lands in the east that our own people had abandoned; on condition that they should defend them."

"My grandfather says the king betrayed his own people, making that treaty—" said Marc'h, a lanky thirteen-year-old who was the son of Constantine. "He should have killed them all."

"Huh—*your* grandfather started the last Saxon war!" someone else replied.

"Perhaps—" Medraut cut in once more, "but then the land

would have been empty, and these same Northmen you call savages might have come instead, and been much harder to deal with. The Saxons, and the Anglians, are not bad people— I have lived among them, and I know. They become more like us the longer they live in our land."

"They hold a quarter of Britannia," muttered Marc'h. "My grandfather says they will try to gobble down the rest of it one day."

Medraut shook his head. "Not if we are strong and stand together. Not if their kings see an advantage in being our allies. I fought shoulder to shoulder with Icel's son, Creoda, and now he calls me friend."

"The campaign—tell us—" came a babble of voices, and Medraut began his tale. He did not exaggerate, or at least, only a little. The men of Demetia who had ridden with him could disprove any claims that were too extravagant, after all. But he had learned among the Saxons that a man owed it to himself to claim his victories.

"And so I have the gratitude of both the Anglians and the Northmen!" Medraut allowed himself a small smile. "There is still glory to be won without ever leaving Britannia."

"The lord Peretur says that the Picts are sure to start a new war soon," said a young guardsman from Eburacum. "He says if the king does not come back soon, Britannia will be as it was in the time of the Vor-Tigernus, when the princes fought each other and left the land at the mercy of its enemies."

"It is true," Medraut said thoughtfully. "We need a strong king, who will put Britannia first. . . ." He stopped, seeing a sudden doubt in some of their faces, while others nodded agreement. Had he meant to hint at rebellion? He hardly knew himself, but the seed was planted now.

"And what if Artor does not come back? What if he and your brothers and all the experienced fighting men are killed by the Franks?" Martinus cried.

"We still have the queen—" answered Medraut. "During these past years, will any deny that she has governed well?"

"But she cannot lead an army—"

"Perhaps not, though I seem to remember that the queens

of our people did just that, when the Romans were conquering this land. But she does not need to. I come from the North, where they still understand that the queen is the source of sovereignty. If the high king falls, or fails, it is for Guendivar to choose a lord to lead this land."

BÎTTER HARVESt

A.D. 514

THE YEARLY LEVIES OF GOLD AND GRAIN WERE DUE AT THE
end of summer, when the corn harvest was in. Each year since
the king had departed, it seemed to Guendivar, the totals had
diminished. Were the princes lying in their reports, or had
Artor's absence really drained the fertility from the land? In
the North, folk held that the soil's productivity depended on
the queen. That was no help, she thought, staring at the
smoke-stained plaster of the wall. How could the land be fe-
cund when the queen was barren?

"Do you have the tally from Dumnonia?" asked Medraut
from the other side of the room.

"Such as it is—" she answered. "According to this, there is
scarcely a stalk of grain in Kernow, and hardly a fish in the
sea." She leaned from her chair to hand him the scroll.

Putting another table in the room for him to use had made
for cramped quarters, but Guendivar did not grudge it. Medraut had a sharp brain, and his mother, whatever his feelings
about her might be, had trained him well. In the past year he
had turned into an able assistant.

And now he was more necessary than ever. The queen felt
her eyes filling with remembered sorrow. For the past year

Cai had insisted on continuing to work even when it was clear he was in pain, and just after midsummer his noble heart had given way at last. She still missed his dour, steady support, but at least Medraut was taking on some of his labor.

"You cannot blame the Dumnonians for wishing to keep their harvest for their own use when they know that what they give us will go to support a war across the sea," he said then.

"Can't they see the need?" Guendivar exclaimed.

"To a farmer in Kernow or a sheepherd in the Lake Country, Gallia seems very far away—"

"I'm sure the Armoricans thought the Franks were distant too," Guendivar replied tartly, "but now they are at their gates. It does not need a Merlin to prophesy that if the Franks are not stopped in Gallia, one day the cliffs of Dubris may see their sails."

"But not today—" repeated Medraut, "and this day, this harvest, is what the people see. They do not understand why their king has abandoned them. They cannot share his dreams."

"What can I do?" She shook her head despairingly. The changes had been slow, and small, but each day the king was away from his kingdom, the web of obligation and loyalty that had held Britannia together frayed a little more. "How can I make them understand?"

"It is Artor's dream!" he exclaimed, rising. "Let *him* persuade them. It is not fair to lay this burden on you!"

"At least this is something I *can* do for him," Guendivar said sadly.

"And this is something I can do for you..." Medraut replied.

Guendivar felt a gentle touch on her shoulder, and then his strong fingers kneading, banishing the tension that knotted the muscles there. She gave an involuntary sigh, leaning into the pressure of his hands. She had not realized how tightly she had been braced against the demands of each day.

"Is that better?" he said softly.

"Wonderful ... where did you learn to do this?"

There was a silence, while he pressed the points that would release the tensions at the base of her neck.

"My mother also was a ruling queen, although, unlike you, she lusted after power. But after a day among the accounts she too grew stiff and sore. She taught me how to massage the pain away. In the evenings I would stand behind her, as now I stand behind you, while her harper played."

"She taught you well. . . ."

"Oh indeed." His voice grew bitter. "She taught me many things . . ." For a moment his grip was almost painful. She made a stifled sound of protest and he grew gentle again.

"What did Morgause do, to hurt you so?" Guendivar asked at last.

"Sometimes I think her first sin was to give birth to me. But no child hates its life. She was my whole world, then." He sighed. "And I believed that I was hers. I knew she favored me more than my brothers. She kept me always by her, directing my every step, and thought, and word. I loved her— I had no one else to love."

"Was that so bad? Or did she change?"

"Change? Not until it was too late for me," Medraut replied. "When I began to feel a man's urges, she took me to the Picts. There were a number of boys of my age there— they showed us a beautiful girl and said she should choose as her lover the lad who did best in the games. She had amber hair like yours," he added softly, "but she was wearing one of my mother's gowns. I know now that it was all arranged beforehand, but at the time I thought her a princess, whom I had won in fair competition with the other boys.

"And perhaps I would have!" he burst out then. "I was skillful and strong. I did well! But after that night, in which I discovered the joy that men find in women's arms, she confessed that she was only a slavegirl, and that she had been told which boy to choose. She wept in my arms, my little Kea, for by then she loved me, and I believed that I loved her, too.

"I begged my mother to buy her for me, but she said the girl was bestowed elsewhere. It was more than a year before I found out that my mother had already purchased Kea herself and ordered her strangled before we had even arrived back at Dun Eidyn."

"But why?" exclaimed Guendivar.

"The reason given was that she must never open to another the womb that had received my first seed! I think that my mother saw how I loved Kea, and feared a rival. . . . But by the time I found out what had happened, Morgause no longer cared whether I loved her. She had left me and whatever plot she had meant to use me in, and run back to her own mother at the Isle of Maidens. I came south, hoping to find better treatment at the hands of my father. But he has abandoned me too, just as he abandoned you!"

"Oh, Medraut!" she exclaimed, half turning. "I am so sorry!"

For a moment the knowing fingers stilled. "Poor little queen . . . so beautiful and wise. She cares for everyone else, but who will care for her?" He began to work again, stroking down along her arms, massaging the muscles of forearm and hand, especially the right, cramped from long hours with sty- lus and quill.

"Such a fair white hand—it doesn't deserve such labor—" He turned it over and began very gently to explore the coun- tours of the palm.

Guendivar shivered. He stood very close, his arms curved around her. It seemed natural to lean against him, savoring the warm strength of the male body that supported her own.

"It deserves . . . to be kissed—" Medraut lifted her hand and gently pressed his lips to the sensitive center of her palm.

"Oh!" She pulled her hand away, still quivering from the jolt of energy that had passed through her body at his touch. "It tickles—" she stammered, stiffening.

Medraut said nothing, but the strong hands drifted back up to her shoulders, gentling her like a nervous mare, and then to her neck and scalp. She relaxed once more, the dangerous moment past.

"You spoke of a plot. What did Morgause plan? I know she did not intend your conception," she said then.

Again, for a moment, the clever fingers stilled. "Not my conception, but from the hour of my birth she raised me to

be her puppet on Artor's throne, because he had stolen Igierne's love, and because she knew the princes of Britannia
would never accept her as queen. Now, of course, she is the
holy Lady of the Lake herself, and would never dream of
disloyalty—"

He drawled out the words with bitter irony.

"And you?" Guendivar said softly.

"I was brought up to serve a queen. You are my lady
now. . . ." Gently he stroked her hair. She sat, half-tranced as
his hands moved down to caress her cheek, turning her head
as he came around to kneel beside her, and reached to kiss
her lips.

His mouth was sweet and warm. She trembled, feeling her
blood leap in answer, and his hand tightened, drawing her
closer. Now his lips claimed what they had only requested
before. Guendivar stiffened, and he let her go.

"I am your father's wife . . ." she whispered.

"But not my mother—" he said thickly. "This, at least, is
not incest."

She straightened, taking a deep breath to slow her pulse.
"Soon, Artor will return. I will keep faith with him."

"But what if he breaks faith with you? What if he never
returns?" Medraut's gaze held hers.

"He will come back!" she said desperately. "Help me, Medraut, I need you. But between us there can be nothing more."

Medraut sat back on his heels, his expression relaxing to
its usual look of irony. "Lady, I will remember. . . ."

The queen turned back to her papers, though she did not
see them, knowing that she would remember as well.

When the first chill winds of fall plucked leaves from the
trees and gleaned the stubbled fields, the princes of Britannia
went hunting. It had become Guendivar's custom, in the
years of Artor's absence, to progress through the kingdom
during the time between harvest and midwinter, allowing her
household to enjoy the sport, renewing acquaintance with the
chieftains, and collecting any taxes that were still in arrears.
This year it was Dumnonia whose contribution was still lack-
ing, and so it was that at the Turning of Autumn the royal

household found itself at Caellwic, an old hillfort south of Din Tagell that Constantine used as a hunting lodge.

The stags were in rut already. The woodland rang with their bellowing. Men stopped when they heard that harsh music, listening, and Medraut recognized the excitement that pulsed in his own veins in the glitter of other men's eyes.

"Go—" said Constantine, who was prevented by a twisted knee from riding. "It is clear that until you have had your sport no one will have any patience for sitting in council. I only wish I could go with you!"

They set out early the next morning, guided by a little dark fellow called Cuby who reminded Medraut of the hidden people of the northern hills. Several of the riders had brought dogs with them, lean grey sight-hounds that strained at their tethers and curly-haired brachets that could follow a blood trail all the way to Annuen.

"A stag—you get now, while still has flesh—" The little man laughed softly. "Wears self to bone, rutting and fighting. This time o'year, thinks with his balls!"

"Like you, Ebi—" said Martinus of Viroconium to one of his friends.

The young man in question flushed. He had acquired a reputation second only to Gualchmai's for affairs with women, and since the latter's marriage, might even have surpassed him.

"And why not?" said someone else in a lower tone. "We must prove our manhood in bed if we are not allowed to do so in war!"

Medraut smiled without speaking, paying more attention to the tone than the words. The men who had come out with him were mostly of his own generation, sons of chieftains, or of men who had gone with Artor over the sea. He watched how they rode and handled their weapons, considering which of them he might want to add to the guard with which he had garrisoned Camalot.

They came down off the high moorland into a wooded valley and their guide held up a hand for silence. Medraut leaned back, gripping hard with his knees as his mount slid down the bank. Somewhere ahead he could hear the gurgle of a stream. His pony threw up its head, snorting, and he reined in hard as half a dozen dark heads popped up from among the hazels. They spoke to Cuby in a soft gabble, and the guide turned back to the riders with a grin.

"They say there is fine deer in meadow downstream. You go carefully, bows ready, and they drive him."

One of the dogs whined and was hushed. The hounds pulled at their leashes, quivering, knowing that soon they would be freed to run.

"Very well," said Medraut. He turned to the other riders. "Mark your targets as you will, but the king stag belongs to me!"

He kicked his mount into the lead. They moved off through the autumn woods, dappled with the golden shadows of the turning leaves. The riders, wrapped in hunting mantles chequered in the earth tones of natural wool, seemed to blend into the branches. Fallen foliage deadened the horses' footfalls; only a soft rustle accompanied their progress, with the squeak of saddle leather and the occasional chink of steel.

There was a tense moment when Martinus reined his mount in hard and it squealed. Medraut rounded on him, frowning, and Martinus pointed to the black-and-white ripple of an adder winding away among the leaves. Martinus was notorious for his fear of serpents; hopefully they would not encounter another. Medraut sighed, and motioned him to move on.

Presently the trees began to thin. Beyond them he glimpsed the meadow, and the red-brown shapes of deer. He reined back and lifted a hand to alert the others, then loosened his rein. His mount took a few steps forward, paused to snatch a mouthful of greenery, then moved on. Through the veil of leaves he saw one of the deer lift its head, ears swiveling, and then, sensing only the random movements of grazing quadrupeds, return to its own meal.

Slowly the hunting party moved through the wood, men peeling off at Medraut's signal to tie their mounts to trees and ready their bows. They could see the deer clearly now, grazing at the other end of the meadow— seven soft-eyed does and the stag who was courting them, his flanks a little ragged, but his head upheld proudly beneath its antler crown. The old king of the forest he was, a stag of twelve tines who had survived many battles and begotten many fawns.

Ho, old man, thought Medraut, *you are looking for the young stag who will try to steal your does. But the creature that comes against you now will take not only your females but land and life itself! Beware!*

The does were grazing, but the stag stood with head up, nostrils flaring as he tested the wind. He was clearly uneasy, but the random movements of the horses had deceived him, and the scent he was seeking was that of his own kind. Medraut saw the edge of the wood before him and reined his own mount in. Moving slowly, he slid from the saddle, using the body of the horse to hide his own from view. With equal care he unslung his bow and nocked an arrow.

A two-legged shape flickered in and out of view at the other end of the meadow. Among the deer, heads jerked up. They began to move, alerted, but not yet alarmed.

Come here, my king . . . thought Medraut, *this way. Your life belongs to me!*

Again the half-seen movement. Now the wind must be bringing scent as well, for a doe jumped to one side. The others stiffened and the stag's heavy head swung round. In another moment they would flee. Medraut lifted the bow, his own muscles quivering with strain.

Off to his left someone sneezed. The deer exploded into motion. Medraut, his gaze fixed on the stag, turned as it leaped forward, awareness narrowing to the gleam of red hide. He felt the arrow thrum from between his fingers, saw it sink into the shining flank, then the stag flashed past him and crashed off through the trees.

He jerked the rein free and flung himself onto his horse's back. A grey shape hurtled past him, barking excitedly. From behind him, hunting horns sounded the chase in bitter harmony. Medraut dug his heels into the pony's sides and sent it after, lips peeled back in a feral grin.

The minutes that followed were a confusion of thrashing leaves and whipping branches. His shot had been a good one, but the stag was strong, and by the time blood loss began to slow him he was halfway down the valley.

Medraut heard a furious yammering of dogs and slapped his pony's neck with the reins. Through the trees he saw a plunging shape, red and brown as it passed through sunlight and shade. Five hounds had brought the stag to bay against an outcropping of stone. As Medraut pulled up, he heard hoofbeats behind him and saw Martinus on a lathered mount.

"Over there—" he shouted. "Keep the dogs to their work!"

Martinus nodded and urged his horse forward, sounding the death on his horn and encouraging the hounds with yips and cries. Medraut had dismounted and tied his own mount, and was working his way around the side, pulling the short hunting sword from its sheath. He heard other riders arriving, but none would dispute his claim. He eased around the tumbled rocks, calculating his approach.

The hart, wheeling to face the darting dogs, was oblivious to its danger. One dog was bleeding from a gashed flank already, and as Medraut crept closer, the stag's head dipped and it hooked another, yelping, into the air. Medraut darted forward, slashing at the tendon that ran down the hind leg, leaping back as the beast lurched, three-legged, towards him.

For a moment he met the white-rimmed gaze, furious and disdainful even now. Then the antlers scythed downward in a wicked slash.

Medraut leaped sideways, aiming for the spot behind the shoulder where a swift stab could pierce upward to the heart. But the stag was faster. Twelve blades blurred towards him. He dropped his sword and threw himself forward, under the tines, then jumped, grabbing the beast's neck and jerking up his legs to avoid the striking hooves.

Overbalanced, the stag fell. Medraut, pinned beneath it, twisted an arm free to draw his dagger, stabbing. His body strained against that of the deer in a desperate embrace, his face jammed against the rank hide, until with a last spasm the stag gave up the battle and lay still.

"My lord! Lord Medraut!"

Dimly, he heard the cries. He struggled to sit up as men pulled the carcass off of him. He got to his feet, amazed to

find nothing broken, though battered limbs were already beginning to complain. The neck of the hart was a bloody mess,
its eyes already dull. He kicked the body and raised his arms,
red to the elbow.

"The old king is dead!" he cried, his voice shrill with release. "The victory is mine!"

In the eyes of the men around him he saw relief, and wonder, and a feral excitement that matched his own. They began
to cry out his name as horns belled victory. In that moment,
the forest, and the dead deer, and the shouting hunters were
one. He looked at them and felt a visceral jolt of connection,
as if the spirit of the stag had entered him. *They are mine!* he
thought. *This land is mine! I claim it as a conqueror!*

Bitter as memory, the music of the horns was carried by
the wind from the tree-choked valley to the bare high moorland that looked over the sea. Merlin paused to listen, the
sprig of thyme forgotten in his hand.

"Medraut has made his kill," said Ninive. "Tonight there
will be venison for the table."

"I would that were all that Medraut brought with him—"
The words came from somewhere below Merlin's conscious
awareness.

"What do you mean?" asked the girl, her fair hair lifting in
the breeze.

Merlin shrugged, knowing neither what he feared nor from
whence the knowledge came.

Eyes narrowing, she gestured towards the plant in his
hand. "You said you would teach me. This lore of herbs and
healing I could learn at the Isle of Maidens. But you are the
prophet of Britannia—teach me how to *know*. . . . "

He spread his hands helplessly, letting the thyme fall to the
ground. Standing with her face uplifted to the sky, Ninive
seemed made of light, her pointed features one with the face
of the daimon that lived within his soul.

"How can I teach you? You *are* knowledge."

"When you look at me, what do you see? And what do I
see when I look at you?" She gave him a long, enigmatic look.
"What you cannot say, perhaps you can show—" she said

softly. Then her voice sharpened. "Speak, O man of wisdom. In the name of your daimon I conjure you. How goes it with the high king in Gallia?"

Merlin felt the first wave of vertigo and gripped the shaft of the Spear with both hands, thrusting the point into the earth as if to root it there. Vision came and went in waves, so he closed his eyes, feeling the ashwood shaft in his hands become the trunk of a great tree mighty enough to uphold worlds. Supported by its strength, he relinquished his attempt to hold onto normal consciousness and let his spirit soar.

In the first moments, awareness extended, borne on the wings of the wind. Below him tossed the grey waves of the sea. Then vision began to focus; he saw hacked woodlands and broad fields trampled to mud where armies had passed. In the dim distance where he had left his body, a voice called his name. He knew that he answered, but not what he said to her.

There was the smoke of a burned village; the air trembled with the echo of battle. Awareness focused further; he saw the standard of the Pendragon and men in battered Roman armor locked in a struggle against big, fairhaired men in high-peaked spangenhelms with gilded figures of eagles glittering from their shields.

He saw Artor bestriding the body of Gwyhir, hewing Franks with mighty strokes until Gualchmai clove a way through the tangle to stand with him. Horns blared, and a wedge of cavalry bore down upon the fray, Betiver in the lead. The Franks fell back then, running towards the mounts they had left at the edge of the field. Betiver pursued. The long Roman lances stabbed and more blood fed the ground.

The scene changed then. It was sunset, and within a circle of torches he could see the body of an old man, wrapped in a purple mantle and laid upon a pyre. Artor took a torch from one of the soldiers and plunged it between the logs, then stood back, the flicker of light gilding the hard planes of his face, as the fire caught the oil-soaked wood and blazed high.

Men crowded around him. One held a cloak like the one that had wrapped the corpse. Artor was shaking his head, but they cast the purple across his shoulders. Others surged forward, shields on their arms, and knelt as the king, still protesting, was lifted. Cheering, they raised him on their shields. Merlin could see mouths opening in unison, heard the echo of their shouting in his soul—*"Imperator! Imperator!"*

Awareness recoiled in a whirl of purple and flame, and he opened his eyes, gasping in the red light of the dying day.

"The king—" he croaked, and coughed, trying to sort through the maelstrom of fading images. "What did I say?"

"Riothamus is dead," said Ninive in a shaken voice, "and they have acclaimed Artor as emperor. . . ."

The Isle of Afallon lay wrapped in the dreaming peace of autumn. Guendivar sat beside the Blood Spring, watching yellow leaves swirl slowly across the pool.

"He will never return, Julia," she said sadly. "I feel it in my heart. If they have made Artor emperor, he has his desire. Why should he return to me, or to Britannia?"

"If you can trust the sorcerer's vision," observed the other woman a trifle grimly. The years had changed Julia little, save for the white veil of a sworn nun that covered her cropped hair. "Every day, it seems, we hear a new tale. Some say that it was Artor, not Riothamus, who died."

Guendivar shook her head. "He is not dead. I would know. . . ."

"Because you are his wife?" Julia lifted one eyebrow. "He has never truly been a husband to you."

"Because I am Artor's queen," corrected Guendivar, "and the land itself would break into lamentation if he departed this world."

Julia snorted disbelievingly. "After ten years does the land even remember him? It is you, my dear one, who are the source of sovereignty. What will you do?" After the death of Mother Madured, the nuns had chosen Julia to lead them, and she spoke with authority.

"Theodoric has sent a ship to Aquilonia for news. I will decide when we know for sure—"

"If you have time!" Julia rose to her feet, shaking her head. "Artor has been too long away, and Britannia is humming like a hive. If he does not come back himself along with the messenger, he may find that the land has given herself else-where! But whatever happens, my queen, remember that there will always be a place for you at Afallon."

Guendivar tried to smile. Once she had thought this isle a prison, but now she could appreciate the power that lay be-neath its peace. All the disciplines of the nuns barely allowed them to endure the energies that pulsed in the chill waters of the spring. She leaned over the water, seeing her own face as a design in flowing planes amid the spiral flow of the current. She dipped up water and the image dislimned, forming anew in the shining drops that fell from her hands.

Both women turned at the sound of a step on the stones. It was one of the novices, still nervous before the queen of Bri-tannia.

"Lady, the lord Medraut would speak with you. . . ."

"He cannot come here," Julia began, but Guendivar was already rising.

"Tell him to join me in the orchard," she said, pulling the veil up over her hair.

The apples had been harvested, and the leaves were falling. Only a few wizened fruits, too small to be worth the effort to reach them, still clung to the highest boughs. But though the trees were bare, they were not barren, for with the new year they would flower and fruit once more.

Unlike me . . . the queen thought bitterly. She paced between the trees and turned, frowning, as Medraut shut the gate and came towards her. Lean and well-knit, with the sunlight bur-nishing his auburn hair, at least he did not remind her of Artor.

"The horses are ready. If we would reach Camalot before dark, we must go now."

"Why should I go back? If Artor does not return, I am no longer queen." Guendivar could feel the kingdom crumbling around her, or perhaps it was she herself who was drying up and flakng away. Medraut caught her by the shoulder as she started to turn.

"Guendivar!" His grip tightened. "You are the source of

sovereignty! Britannia needs you—*I* need you! My lady, my beloved, don't you understand?"

She retreated, shaking her head, and he followed, still holding her, until her back was against a tree.

"Guendivar.... Guendivar...." He pulled the veil from her head and, very gently, touched her hair. "You are source and the center, the wellspring and the sacred grove."

She stood, scarcely breathing, as his hand moved from her hair to her cheek. This was not the disguised seduction he had tried before. Gentle he might be, but there was an authority in his grip that she could not deny. She turned her head, but he forced it back again, and then he was kissing her, hard and deep, and she felt the power begin to leave her limbs.

"Artor is gone..." he murmured into her hair. "He has abandoned us, and without a king, the princes will tear this poor land apart like wolves. I can lead them, I know it, but only you can legitimate my rule!"

His hand slid down her neck, pushing the tunica from her shoulder to cup her breast, and she began to tremble, long-supressed responses flaming into awareness once more.

"Guendivar ... Guendivar.... Marry me, and I will love you as he never could. I know how to serve a queen!" He bowed before her, hands sliding down her sides until he knelt, holding her against him, head pressed against the joining of her thighs.

"I am your father's wife ..." she whispered, fighting to stay upright. If once he got her on her back upon the grass, she would have no power to stop whatever he might do.

And why am I resisting? she wondered. When had Artor ever come to her with such passion, such need?

"He has renounced the marriage, and you are no kin to me—" he said thickly. "Come to me, Guendivar, give me the right to rule...."

"Not here ..." she whispered. "This is holy ground...."

Medraut leaned back a little, gazing up at her with darkened gaze. "But you will lie with me, won't you, my dearest? You will marry me?"

Guendivar shuddered, her body aching with need. It was

too late, she thought. She had no choice, now—she had already given too much away. Without volition, the words came to her. "When you are king. . . ."

The queen sat in her place in the round Council Hall, an image of sovereignty draped in cloth of gold. Medraut had taken his seat on the other side of the king's empty chair.

Soon, he thought, *it will be* my *chair!* As soon as the men he had summoned to his Midwinter Feasting agreed. . . . The blazing fire in the center of the circle flickered on faces sharpened by interest, glinted on the softness of fur lined mantles and the glint of gold. The houseposts were wreathed with evergreen, set with holly and ivy and mistletoe.

To call them together had been a risk, he knew. It might have been safer to simply proclaim himself king. If Artor had left the Sword behind, Medraut could have proved his right by pulling it from the stone. His mother had explained the trick of it, and he was of the blood—twice over, he thought with a sardonic grin.

But he could call himself Basileus of Byzantium, or lord of the Blessed Isles, and it would mean nothing if no one followed him. He must be acclaimed by the princes of Britannia, or by enough of them to impress the remainder. Camalot was garrisoned with men he had chosen. He had sent word already to Aelle and Cynric and Icel, and knew that they would send him warriors when he called. But to rule Britannia, he needed the support of these men.

He gazed around the chamber, counting those of whom he was certain, and those he judged weak enough to be swayed. There were some, like Theodoric in Demetia and Eldaul of Glevum, whom he knew would accept no heir until they saw Artor in his grave. The invitations sent to them had all—so sorry—gone astray. Of the older men, he had only Cataur of Dumnonia, who had never been Artor's friend, with his son Constantine by his side.

But Martinus of Viroconium, newly succeeded to his father's seat, would stand behind him, and so would Caninus of Glevum, whatever his father might say. The boys from Guenet, Maglouen and Cunoglassus, though young, came of noble kin. Where the sons were seduced by dreams of glory, the fathers might be persuaded by lower taxes and a more accommodating authority.

Medraut waited, poised as the hawk that hovers over the field, until all had taken their places, waited until the silence was becoming uncomfortable, before he got to his feet in an easy movement that focused their attention. He had dressed with care in a long tunic of Byzantine brocade dyed a crimson so deep it was almost purple. His black cloak was lined with wolfskin. Around his neck glinted a king's torque of twisted gold.

"Lords of Britannia, I bid you welcome. It is the queen who has called you here to council, as is her right. I speak in her name—" He bowed to Guendivar, who inclined her head, her features as expressionless as those of a Roman statue beneath the veil.

"And why does she—or you—summon us here?" Cataur called out in reply.

"To take counsel for the future of this island, for ten long years bereft of her king." He waited for the murmur to subside.

"Have you had word of Artor's death?" asked Paulinus of Viroconium.

"We have had rumors only. There was a great battle with the Franks, and many were killed. My informants saw a funeral pyre and were told that the Britons were burning their king."

The outbreak of response to this was sharper. Many here had resented Artor's rule, but he had also been much loved. Guendivar looked up abruptly at his words, for she believed the confused tale of Merlin's prophecy, that it was Riothamus who had died.

"Perhaps he is not dead"—he shrugged—"although I do not understand why, if Artor lives, he has not sent word. Perhaps they have made him emperor, and he no longer cares for Britannia." Medraut spread his hands. "My lords—does it really matter? He is not here! Is that the act of a lord who cares for his people?" he exclaimed.

"The season of storms is on us, bad for sailing," said some-one, but the rest of the men were shouting agreement.

"Is that the way of a Defender of the land? The way of a king?" Medraut continued, drawing more shouts with each repetition.

He moved away from his seat and began to pace around the circle. "Last year men from the North attacked the coast of Anglia. I led a troop of British warriors, and rode with Icel's son Creoda to defeat them. We parted in friendship, but do you think the Anglians did not notice that Britannia has no king to defend her? They accepted me only because I am King Artor's . . . kin."

Medraut saw eyes flickering towards his face and away again. They had become accustomed to him—time to remind them who he really was.

"I spent nearly nine years among the Saxons, and learned their tongue. After a time they forgot to watch their words around me. They are quiet now, but they have not given up their dreams of conquering the rest of this isle. For a decade the fear of Artor's name has held them, but a new generation of warriors is growing up who have not learned to respect British arms. Whether by fear or friendship, they must be fettered anew, and this can only be done by a king."

The fire wavered as the pressure inside the hall was changed by a gust of wind outside, as if to echo his words.

"And do you claim the kingship?" cried one of the Dumnonian lords.

Medraut took a deep breath. For this he had been born; he had been trained up by his mother to be her weapon against the king. Now that Morgause had renounced vengeance, to take Artor's place would be his revenge on her. And he wanted it, more than he had ever wanted anything, except perhaps for his mother's love, or Kea, or Guendivar.

"I do. I have the right, whether you count me as son or sister-son, and I have the will." His voice rang through the hall. "Artor wasted your sons and your wealth in a senseless foreign war. I will keep both safe in Britannia. He kept a tight rein on the princes of this land; but the Saxon wars are long past, and we can afford to rule with less central authority.

There must be one man with the power, and the prestige, to deal with them. All these things I will do as your king!"

"What says the lady Guendivar?" asked Constantine.

Medraut turned to the queen and held out his hand. She rose to her feet, paler, if possible, than she had been before.

"Artor has abandoned us," she said in a low voice. "Let Medraut take the rule. . . ."

He bent before her, then straightened, standing of a purpose where firelight would veil him in gold.

"Medraut!" called Martinus and Cunoglassus, and after them a dozen others took up the cry. They shouted his name till the rafters rang, and when the acclamation died away at last, Medraut sat down in the great carved chair of the king.

BELTAIN FIRES

A.D. 515

ARTOR SPLASHED THROUGH THE ICY WAVES, STRUGGLING TO
keep his feet against the surge, until the tide retreated behind
him. A few more steps and the stony shore was solid beneath
his feet. He sank to his knees, plunging his fingers deep into
the swirled ridges of pebble and sand.

Britannia! For so long, as winter storms lashed the narrow
sea, he had thought he would never get here. But this holy
earth was truly his homeland—it spoke to him as the soil of
Gallia could never do. He bent and kissed the stones.

The ground trembled to the tread of the men and horses
that were struggling ashore all around him. As he straightened again, the mists thinned and he saw the pale glimmer
of the chalk cliffs that flanked the harbor. For two months
they had haunted him, seen first in the dream that had
brought him home. Even now the images made him writhe:
Medraut in the king's high seat, Medraut with his arms
around Guendivar. At first, he had thought the vision some
bastard offspring of his own fears. But the dream had the
flavor of Merlin's power, and as Artor got his men into winter
quarters after that last, triumphant battle, he had begun to

believe it, even before Theodoric's storm-battered galley brought the news.

Medraut had proclaimed himself high king. He held Camalot and Londinium, and Dumnonia stood his ally. He had made his own treaties with the Saxons, and the rest of the Island was on the verge of civil war. And Guendivar had pledged herself to be his queen.

That was the blade that pierced Artor's heart. Until she betrayed him, he had not realized how much of his soul he had given to his queen. He lifted his head, trying to see through the mists. He had half expected to find Merlin waiting for him to come ashore. If the Druid knew enough to warn him, why had he not put a stop to Medraut's treachery?

"My lord! Did you fall?" Goriat's tall form bent beside him.

Artor shook his head, but the damp of the voyage had stiffened his joints, and he accepted a hand to help himself get up again. There was not much left in Goriat of the youth who had once served in the kitchens of Camalot, he thought grimly, except for the innocence in his eyes. He looked much like Gualchmai, both of them hard muscled and fair and taller than the other men, though Gualchmai's sandy hair was laced with silver now. Aggarban and Gwyhir lay in the earth of Gallia. Since hearing the news from Britannia, the two brothers who survived no longer counted Medraut as kin.

"Well, at least there's no enemy here to meet us—" Goriat squinted past the remains of the old fortress of Dubris towards the downs.

Artor nodded. No doubt that was why Merlin had shown him these cliffs in his dream. In the season of storms he dared no longer crossing, and Dumnonia and the lands the south Saxons ruled would be held against him. Only in Cantium could he hope to land unopposed, if Rigana and Eormenric stayed true.

He looked around him, shading his eyes as the pale February sunlight broke through the fog. Shadow shapes of boats darkened the shoreline. The strand was a confusion of horses and men. It was the warriors of Britannia he had with him— the others had been left with Betiver in Gallia. Men fought best for their own land. The sorrow here was that the same might be said of both sides.

"Get the gear unloaded and form up the baggage train. I'll want to meet with troop commanders as soon as possible. We'll march on Cantuwareburh in the morning."

A day later, Artor was sitting in Hengest's hall. The beams were darker, the walls covered by embroidered cloths, but otherwise it was much as he remembered from Oesc's wedding to Rigana, some twenty-one years before. The year before Mons Badonicus, that had been, when Oesc was killed. Rigana's slenderness had become a whipcord strength, her features sharpened by maturity; in appearance, she seemed little changed. He did not think that she had mellowed, though she seemed to have her temper under better control. But Eormenric was grown to manhood, and Artor winced to see his father look out of his eyes.

Oesc, wherever he is now, has more reason to be proud of his son than I do of mine, he thought bitterly.

"Oh yes, Medraut has sent messengers," observed Rigana, as if she had read his thought. "Gifts as well. We smiled, and took them. Why not?" she went on. "There was no point in defiance until we knew your plans—" She untied a soft leather bag from her belt and plopped it in front of Artor with a musical clink of gold.

"What, did you think I still held Oesc's death against you?" Rigana added wryly. "It was Cataur and Ceretic who destroyed him. And the West Seax and the Dumnonians are Medraut's allies." She turned to her son, whose face had changed at the mention of Ceretic's name. "I know you fear to face your friend Ceawlin in battle, but this is the way of the world. When he thought it needful to avenge me, your father went even against Artor, whom he loved. . . ."

The king watched his own fingers clench on his drinking horn until the knuckles whitened, and forced them to release again. "If you will raise the men of your *fyrd* to follow me, under a good commander, I will be grateful," he said harshly. "But you, boy, stay home to guard Cantuware. This conflict has set brother against brother and father against son already. I will not ask you to fight against your friend."

Rigana's gaze softened. "I see you are still capable of mercy. Remember it, when you have the victory."

"Do you think I will win?"

"When the people see that you have come back to them, they will turn to you," she answered him, "save for those who have been driven so far they think no forgiveness is possible."

"You are talking about Medraut, and . . . the queen?" Odd, how he could not say her name.

"Consider this—Guendivar supports his cause, but she has not married him. Leave a way open for her to come to you. . . ."

Artor stared at her, thinking on the things she did not say. Rigana was the Lady of Cantium; she knew the queen could bestow the sovereignty of the land on the man who served her well. Perhaps Guendivar had not yet given herself to Medraut, but he himself had been no use to her either. He recognized now that it was one reason he had stayed away.

"She must hate me—" he whispered, knowing that until he was able to forgive himself, he could not forgive his queen. And until then, he had no choice but to press on with the bloody business of war.

The king's forces marched swiftly through the chill spring rains, taking the old Roman road westward towards Londinium. At Durobrivae their camp was attacked in the hour before dawn by tall, fair men whose sleek ships had crossed the estuary of the Tamesis. By the time they were beaten off, several wagonloads of supplies had been burned and a number of men killed. The one prisoner they took told them he was a Northman from the settlement Gipp had made on the coast of the Anglian lands, and then, laughing, tore off the bandage with which they had stopped his bleeding and died.

The art of making friends with barbarians, thought Artor grimly, was a gift his son seemed to have inherited. But he said nothing, and ordered his army to continue on.

There were several skirmishes before they reached Londinium, but the city was not held against them. There was no need. Medraut had already stripped it of all supplies. Even in Artor's youth the city had been decaying. There was little left of it now. Still, it was good to take shelter beneath such roofs as remained intact while the king's scouts tried to find out which way the enemy had gone. There he found Betiver's son by the Votadini girl who for nearly twenty years had been his concubine. To have the young man at his side was some small consolation for having had to leave Betiver with the rest of his troops in Gallia.

Thus, it was the middle of the month of Mars before word came that the rebel forces were gathering near Ambrosiacum on the great western plain.

Medraut stood before the Mound of the Princes, watching his father's army form up across the plain. They were armed, as were his own forces, but had not put on their helmets. Artor had called for a parley. Medraut wondered if it could possibly succeed. A chill wind rustled the husks of last year's grass and ruffled the new blades of green, its force scarcely checked by the ancient stones of the Giant's Dance, and he refastened his wolfskin cloak above his mail.

He had not done so badly, he thought, looking over his men. The South and much of the West had declared for him, and those few who resisted, like Eldaul of Glevum, had been overcome. But except for a few skirmishes, the rebels had not yet faced Artor's army, and the old king's reputation was worth a legion. It was Constantine who had insisted that they try negotiation now.

Medraut wondered whether he was confused by old loyalties or simply afraid. Artor's men might be veterans, thought Medraut as he watched uneasily, but they were *old;* experienced they might be, but their strength had been worn away in the Gallian campaigns. He told himself there was no need to fear.

The wind died, and Medraut looked over his shoulder, seized by the odd sense that the spirits in the mound were watching him. He smiled sardonically. They must be very confused. A war of Briton against Briton would be familiar enough, but behind Artor marched Jutes from Cantuware, while Saxons led by Cynric and Cymen and Anglians under Creoda rode in his own train.

The movement before him shivered to stillness. From Artor's army a horn blew shrill, to be answered after a moment from his own side. Constantine of Dumnonia stepped forward, his thinning hair blowing in the breeze. From Artor's side, the spokesman was Gualchmai, grim-faced and frowning, limping a little from some wound got in the Gallian wars. There was a murmur of disbelief from the Dumnonians when they saw him come forward. If the king had sent Gualchmai, it was not to negotiate, but to deliver terms.

Gualchmai halted, his thumbs hooked through his belt, surveying the enemy. Medraut flinched at the chill in his brother's blue gaze.

"So, we are standing together. If I had my will, I'd answer the boasts of your little prince with a good hiding, but I am bound to hear ye out, so say on—"

"My lord Medraut..." Constantine coughed to stop his voice from wavering, "requires that the high king give him the North to govern and recognize him as heir to Britannia."

"Fine words for a rebel!" growled Gualchmai. "My lord king requires first that Medraut return his lady and queen. After that, he may find the patience to receive your surrender!"

"Surrender?" Constantine tried to laugh. "When our army outnumbers yours?"

"We've beaten the Franks, who smashed every other army that faced them. D'ye think we'd have any trouble with yours?"

"It is a hard thing, when brother fights brother..." Constantine said piously. "And in any case, it is not for us to dispose of the Lady Guendivar—the choice of where she should go is hers."

The queen had been left in the care of a household of holy women who had settled at Ambrosiacum, and even Medraut did not know what she would do. Sometimes the aching tenderness with which he courted her gave way to visions in which he held that smooth white body splayed beneath him, victim of his desire. But he was too much his mother's son to dare to force her. He had felt her need for him—surely he was the one she would choose!

"Promise the prince a territory to govern and his place as heir, and we will disband," Constantine went on.

Let me have the North, thought Medraut, *and Artor will have to face Cynric and Cymen here. . . .* It would be good to get back to his own country. Once across the Wall he would be dealing with folk who had never really accepted the rule of Britannia. And beyond them waited the Picts, allies even more powerful than the Saxon tribes.

Artor nodded, and Gualchmai turned to Constantine with a sigh. "Let it be so."

But not for long, thought Medraut. Artor had not met his gaze, but in the grey light he could see the lines in the older man's face and the silver in his hair. He remembered how the stag had gasped out its life beneath his blade. *You are old, my father—and soon my time will come.*

"We'll drink together to seal the bargain," the Dumnonian replied, "and our lords shall swear to keep faith on the holy cross." Young Maglocun brought out a silver-banded horn filled with ale, and Father Kebi was pushed forward across the grass with crucifix in hand, eyeing the warriors around him like a wether among wolves.

On both sides, the men moved forward, the better to see. And at that moment, someone yelled and steel flashed in the sun. Every head turned. Medraut saw Martinus' face contort in disgust, and a flicker of black-and-white in the grass. The bare blade in his hand lifted, stained with red.

But a greater light was already flaring from the wheeling arc of Gualchmai's sword. "Treachery!" he cried, and then he clove Martinus through the shoulder and struck him down.

For an instant longer Medraut stared. The scene had shattered like a broken mosaic, horns blaring, men running everywhere. Then Cunoglassus pulled him back, shoving helm and shield into his hands. He fumbled to fix the straps, saw Cymen with his houseguard forming a shieldwall, and ran towards its protection.

*   *   *

In the years that came after, few could tell the true story of that deadly, confused conflict before the ancient circle of stones; a battle begun without plan and ending in darkness, with no clear victor. Folk knew only that more blood dyed the plain that day than had ever moistened the pagan altar stone. When it was over, the remnants of Medraut's army marched northward. From that time, news of the war came to the Britons of the South only as rumors that blended to create an imagined reality.

But to Artor, searching the battlefield with flickering torch in hand, it was all too real. Though most of the fallen came from the ranks of his foes, the toll among the men he had brought back from Gallia was heavy as well. He moved among the heaped bodies, recognizing here a man who had saved his life in Armorica, and there a fellow who had always been able to make his comrades laugh.

And near the hour of midnight, when the flesh grows cold on the bones, he found Gualchmai.

The king saw first the corpses, heaped in a distorted circle as if some dark elf had tried to construct a hillfort from the bodies of the slain. He had seen such ramparts before, where some brave soldier had stood at bay, but never so high. He was still staring at it when Goriat came up to him.

"Have you found your brother?" Artor asked, and Goriat shook his head. "Well, perhaps we should look there—" the king said then, indicating the heap of slain.

Wordless, Goriat handed Artor his torch and began to drag the bodies aside. They had fallen in layers—Icel's Anglians atop men from Dumnonia, and beneath them warriors from Cynric's band, all slain by the strokes of a sword. When Goriat had cleared a narrow pathway, Artor followed him to the center. Gualchmai lay there in a pool of red, the great sword still clenched in his hand. No single warrior could have killed him—it was loss of blood from too many wounds that had felled him at last.

"I used to dream of surpassing him," whispered Goriat. "But no warrior will ever enter Annuen with such a noble escort as these."

Artor nodded agreement, then stiffened as Gualchmai

stirred. In the next moment he was kneeling beside him, feeling for a pulse beneath the blood-stiffened beard.

"Gualchmai, lad, can you hear me?" He cradled his nephew's head on his lap, stroking his brow. "Goriat, go for a wagon, bring blankets and water, run!" Gualchmai's flesh was cold, but his chest still rose and fell.

"Artor. . . ."

He could barely hear the whisper of sound. "Hush, lad, I am here."

"My fault . . . it was an adder . . . I saw . . . as my sword fell. . . . I have paid."

"Gualchmai, you must live," Artor said desperately. "I loved you and Betiver best of all in the world. Without you, how can I survive?"

Perhaps it was a trick of the torchlight, but he thought Gualchmai's lips curved in a smile. "The king . . . will never die. . . ."

When Goriat and the others arrived, Artor was still sitting with Gualchmai's head pillowed on his thigh, but on the king's cheek they could see the glistening track of tears, and they knew that the champion of Britannia was gone.

"My lord, what shall we do now?"

"Bury Gualchmai in the Mound of the Princes, and dig a grave for the rest of our folk who have fallen here," said Artor. From his eyes the tears still flowed, but his voice was like stone. "Where is the enemy?"

"The Dumnonians are scuttling westward like rats to their holes, but Medraut has gone north," answered Goriat. "They say he has taken the queen and the lady Ninive."

"Then north we shall go as well. Whether he flees to Alba or to Ultima Thule, there is no place on this earth so distant that I will not follow him."

By the day, the air rang with the sound of adze and hammer as Medraut's soldiers rebuilt the palisade of Dun Bara, the fort on the hill. Escorted, Guendivar paced the old earthworks, Ninive beside her. Battered and bruised by the pace of their journey northward, she had prayed only for its ending, but as her body recovered, she began to realize how small was the difference between prize and prisoner.

Beyond the half-built walls she could see a long sweep of hill and moorland and a bright glitter of water beyond them. It was the estuary of the Tava, they had told her. On the other side lay the dark masses of Fodreu. Even the Votadini lands, thought Guendivar as she refastened her cloak, would have seemed strange to her, but Medraut had carried her deep into the country of the Pretani, the Painted People, who had always been the enemies of Britannia. Wind and water tasted different here, and the soil was strange. Here, she was no longer a queen.

Ninive, on the other hand, had grown stronger with every step northward. "My mother was a Royal Woman of the Hidden People, the first folk to inhabit this land," she said, laughing, her fair hair flying in the wind. "I ran wild as a moorland pony until I was eleven years old. Then Gualchmai rode that way out hunting, as he had done when he met my mother and begot me. She was dead by then, and he took me to the Isle of Maidens, to Igierne. Only in this land have I ever been truly free!"

Guendivar shook her head, understanding only that when Medraut ordered her to choose one woman to come with her she had been wise to take Ninive. Had Merlin come north as well? Some of Medraut's men claimed to have seen a Wild Man beyond the flicker of their fires, but if it was the Druid, he had made no attempt to speak with her.

And why should he? she thought bitterly. *I have given him no reason to think I need rescuing. He waits for Ninive, not for me. . . .*

She shivered, and turned towards the roughly thatched hut they had built for the women while they worked on Medraut's hall. It was dark and had few comforts, but at least there was a fire.

That night, Medraut returned, with a band of laughing Pictish warriors, a herd of hairy black cattle, and a line of laden horses. Soon fires were burning and two of the cows were cooking, the large joints roasting over the coals while the rest boiled in crude bags made from their own hides.

For Guendivar he brought a straw-filled mattress and warm woolen blankets, and a mantle of chequered wool in shades of earthy green that he said was a gift from the Pictish queen.

"I am grateful," she said dully when Bleitisbluth, the smooth-tongued Pict who had become Medraut's shadow, had left them, "particularly since I am sure she has no wish to share her land with another queen. This is not my country, Medraut. How long will you keep me here?"

"Is it not?" He grinned whitely, and she realized that he had already had his share of the heather beer. "Pretani is just another word for Briton, and though this land never bowed to Rome, Alba and the south are all part of the same hallowed isle!"

"But these are Picts!" she said in a low voice. "They have always been our enemies!"

"The enemies of the soft southern tribes," he answered, "and the foes of Rome, not mine."

Guendivar could see that was true. Medraut stood now in kilt and mantle chequered in soft ochre and crimson. Of his southern gear he retained only the golden torque. His bare breast was shaded blue with the sinuous spirals of Pictish tatooing, his brow banded with Pictish gold.

"I have endured the rites by which they make a man a warrior. At the feast of Beltain we will swear formal alliance, and I will make for you a wedding feast in the old way that our people followed before ever Christian priest came into this land."

As Medraut's hands closed on her shoulders she stepped backward, but the doorpost was behind her, and there was nowhere to go. She trembled as his mouth claimed hers, feeling even now, as his hands moved over her body, the traitorous leap in the blood.

"Lie with me, Guendivar . . ." he said thickly, his touch growing more intimate. "Open your womb, white lady, and let me possess you utterly. Then I will truly be king!"

"When we are wedded—" she gasped. "I am no use to you if men think me your whore."

For a moment longer he gripped her, until she wondered

if the conflict between lust and logic would break him—or her. Then, with an oath, he jerked away.

"*Wise* Guendivar . . ." he said furiously. "You deny me with such reasonable words. But in half a moon I will have you, spread-eagled on the feasting table if need be, so that all men may see that you are mine!" He thrust her away and pushed through the cowhide that hung across the door.

The fire flared as it flapped shut behind him, and Guendivar sank to her knees, her breath coming in shuddering sobs.

"Help me, Ninive!" she whispered as the younger woman put her arms around her. "What can I do?"

"You want him, don't you . . ." murmured Ninive, helping her to sit down by the fire.

"*Him?*" The queen shivered. "Not now, not anymore. But a man's strength to hold me, that I do—Medraut has lit the fire, damn him, and I burn! You don't understand, do you?" She lifted her head to look at Ninive. "Have you never felt your flesh quicken at the touch of a man?"

The other woman shook her head, her great eyes dark and quiet as forest pools.

"Not even Merlin?" Guendivar asked then.

"The love of the body is not what the Druid wants from me. . . ." Her lips curved in a secret smile.

The queen stared at her, but she had not the strength just now to try to understand. "It does not matter. But if Merlin were here, I would beg him to carry me away. . . ."

"Is that truly your will?" Ninive said slowly.

"Oh, my dear, I have known for moons that Medraut is no true king, but where could I go? Artor may have sworn to retrieve me, but he will not want me back again. Still, I will not weaken him further by joining myself to a man who would destroy Britannia! Better I should die in the wilderness, or live a hermit for the rest of my days, than become Medraut's queen!"

"Eat something, my lady, and rest while you may," said Ninive, her gaze gone inward. "And in the dark hours, when the men lie drunk or sleeping, we shall see. . . ."

Sure that sleep was impossible, Guendivar obeyed, but exhaustion claimed her, and when she roused at last to Ninive's whisper, it was from a dream of the Isle of Apples and the sacred spring.

The hearthfire was cold and the doorflap had been thrust aside. Mist curled through the opening, and when she emerged, wrapped in the Pictish cloak, she could see no more than the snoring shape of little Doli, the Pictish servant whom Medraut had set to guard her. Beyond him rose the bulk of the half-built hall. Then, as if he had precipitated from the mist, another figure was there, tall, swathed in a mantle, leaning on a spear.

He gestured, and Ninive took the queen's arm and drew her after, past men sprawled in sleep and drowsing horses, through the open gate of the fortress and down the hill into the waiting fog.

To Guendivar, it was as if they passed through the mists of the Otherworld. But by morning, her aching legs told her that they had covered many miles. They took refuge in a shallow cave, its entrance hidden by hawthornes whose buds were just on the edge of bloom. Guendivar had barely a moment to long for the Pict-queen's mattress before she fell asleep in Ninive's arms.

The next night also they travelled, though the queen's sore feet and aching muscles would not let her go fast or far. If Medraut had set the Picts to search for her she saw no sign of them, and trusted Merlin's woodcraft to keep their passage unknown. On the third day, he brought them horses—sturdy moorland ponies who could cross rough terrain without injury and would keep on going long after the endurance of a warhorse failed.

They moved south and east through the hills, Merlin pacing like a shadow ahead and beside them. His hair and beard were now entirely silver, but despite his age, he pushed on. Each morning there would be a handful of spring greens and some small creature, a hare or grouse or hedgehog, to cook over their little fire. Where Guendivar was sore and exhausted, Ninive grew lean and hardy, kirtling up her skirts and letting down her hair until she was no longer a royal lady but a woods-colt who could keep pace with Merlin.

On the fifth day of their journey, the pace eased, and they began to travel by day. They had crossed over into the lands of the Votadini, where the Picts would not yet follow. That night, Merlin asked her where she wished to go.

"Artor is on his way northward, though he goes slowly, trying to heal the destruction Medraut wrought as he passed. There is hardly a family that this rebellion has not divided, a thousand sparks that must be stamped out before he can fight the real fire."

"I cannot face him!" Guendivar drew back, trying to read the dark eyes beneath Merlin's bushy brows. He walked now in the skin garments of a Wild Man, the only touch of civilization about him the rune-carved Spear. It seemed to her that from time to time he leaned on it more heavily; that the pace he had set for them during the past days was slower, but she did not dare to ask if he were well.

"If I could choose, I would return to the South, to my own country. Perhaps I could take refuge with the holy women at the Isle of Afallon."

"Do you not understand?" He shook his head. "The choice is always yours—you are the queen."

Guendivar stared at him, tears burning down her cheeks, her throat aching so that she could not say a word.

"But the time for decision is not yet upon us," he went on as if he had not seen. "We will continue south towards the Wall, and perhaps on the journey you will find better counsel."

The days lengthened towards Beltain, and the land began to bloom. Now creamy primroses appeared in sunny patches, and the first bluebells nodded beneath the leafing trees. The moorlands were starred with white heather and budding bilberry. Just so, thought Guendivar, the land had arrayed itself when she rode to her wedding, and wondered if she would ever be done with tears.

They made their way eastward along the shore of the Bodotria, and then turned south to follow the old Roman road. Travel grew easier and she lost count of the days.

And then, one evening as the sun began to sink behind the hills, she heard the faint throb of drums. She kicked the pony into a trot and caught up with Merlin.

"What is it? Is there war?"

He shook his head, smiling oddly. "It is the eve of Beltain. . . ."

"Do you know some warded spot where we will be safe through the dark hours?"

"My child, why are you so frightened? Have you forgotten everything you knew?" He picked an early hawthorne blossom from the hedge and laid it in her hand. "Do not fear—where I lead you we will be welcome."

They rode onward through the long spring dusk. Across the valley she saw three peaks in silhouette against the sky. The drumming came now from one direction, now from another, soft with distance. Ninive had made wreaths for herself and Merlin, out of primrose and fragrant herbs. She held another up to Guendivar, and the queen had already set it on her brow before she realized it was a hawthorne crown.

For a moment Guendivar wanted to throw it down, remembering the wreath that had held her bridal veil. But the air was full of a rich, green smell, and she was no longer the child who had been Artor's bride. *Let them do as they will . . .* she thought with sweet melancholy, *it does not matter what happens to me.*

It was almost dark, but Merlin led them unflagging onto a track that wound across the moor. The western horizon still glowed, but above them, stars were blossoming in the sky. They had come around behind the tall northeastern peak where the remains of earthen ramparts rose, and were approaching the space between the other two hills.

The drumming was much louder. A prickle of fear chilled her.

"Ninive—what is it? Where are we going?"

For a moment the younger woman paused. "Oh my lady, those are the drums of my own people! I did not know that any still lived in these lands!" She ran ahead up the path.

But Merlin took Guendivar's bridle and led the horse up around the curve of the hill, stopping once or twice to catch his breath before pressing on. In the fold between the middle and southern peaks rose a rocky bump, where a bonfire sent sparks whirling up to dance with the stars. Dark figures cavorted around it, clad, like Ninive, who had cast off her tunic and run to join them, only in wreaths of flowers. The dancers clustered around her, chattering in a swift guttural language Guendivar did not know, but as Merlin led her into the circle of firelight they fell silent.

She stared into eyes dark as Ninive's, memory whirling with fragments of fearful tales of the people of the hills. After a long moment, she realized that they were as frightened as she. Merlin spoke then, his deep voice rumbling like an echo of the drums, and the fear changed to wonder. Women pulled heather and covered it with skins to make a seat, and when she slid down from the pony, escorted her there. As the drumming began once more, a small girl shyly offered her a wooden bowl filled with a dark liquid that tasted like honey mixed with fire.

"What did you tell them," she asked Merlin, "to make them welcome me this way?"

He smiled down at her, his hair bright as a snowy peak in the sun. "I told them the truth—I said that I had brought their queen."

She should have been angry, but the mead had lit a fire in her belly, and the drumming was beating in her blood. She looked at him and laughed. If eating this food bound her to the Hidden Realm, perhaps she could forget Artor.

The dancing continued. Guendivar ate roasted meat and dried berries, mixed with other things she did not try to identify. There was always more mead when her bowl emptied, the fire's reflection burning across the surface like liquid gold. She grew warm, and pulled off gown and tunica until she was as naked as the dancers. Men and women jumped together over the fire and wandered off into the darkness, laughing softly. The sighs of their passion whispered in time to the beat of the drums.

In the heavens, the stars were dancing, wheeling across the

sky in patterns ancient when the world was new. She thought it must be near midnight when something in the music began to change.

People were still leaping around the fire, but they were not the same. They had put on the skins of animals, or perhaps they *were* animals, coupling in the compulsion of spring. She blinked, peering through the swirling smoke, and could not tell. Merlin would know, she thought then, but he too had disappeared, or changed. The drumming had a deeper note, as if the earth itself had become a single vibrating skin. That beat throbbed in her belly, bringing her swaying to her feet. From some depths she had never suspected, a sound rose in her throat and burst free in a wordless cry.

All around her, people were joined in the night's ecstasy, exulting in the passion that she had never been free to enjoy— she, whose fulfillment should have renewed them all! Guendivar took a step forward, stretching her arms to the skies.

"Come!" she cried to the night, to the fire, to the earth beneath her feet. "Oh my beloved, in the name of the Lady, come to me!"

And in the moment between one breath and another, from forest and flame and shadow, He came.

Furred like a beast, like a man He walked upright, and the antlers of the king of the wood crowned His brow. Erect, He came to her and bore her away in His strong arms. Filling and fulfilling He served her, pressing her down upon the moist earth, and the passion that until now had lain potential within her welled up in response, and flowed out from her into the land.

Guendivar was awakened in the dawning by the singing of many birds. Warm wool wrapped her, but the grass against her face was chill with dew. She stretched, muzzily aware of a pleasant soreness, and opened her eyes. The Pict-queen's cloak covered her, and her head was pillowed on her folded clothes. She blinked again; the world around her was a delicate dazzle of light. Through the branches of the hawthorne she could see a translucent sky whose banners of cloud were beginning to flush with gold. But each leaf was outlined in its own radiance, and moving among them she glimpsed vortices of whirling light.

She sat up, and clearing vision showed her luminous forms that expanded, as if in response to her attention, until they were the size of children, staring back at her with shining eyes.

"We hail the Queen!" sang the sweet voices. "We hail the Hawthorne Bride! The Lady has come to the land!"

"I know you . . ." whispered Guendivar, looking back in memory at the girl-child who had played with the faerie folk in the woods of the Summer Country long ago. For a moment, her vision blurred. Prisoned within walls, surrounded by humans with all their blind needs, she had forgotten how to see. . . .

"We live between the worlds. Between sunrise and sunset we can fly from one end to the other of this Isle. Will you stay with us, Lady, or will you ride?" Bird song and faerie song mingled in a cascade of harmonies.

"The queen has come to the land, but the king still wanders—" she answered.

Merlin had tried to tell her what was needed, but she had been unable to understand. She looked from the bright spirits to her own flesh—it felt solid, but her skin had a translucent glow, as if she could see the pulse of power.

"Between sunrise and sunset, my fair ones, take me to Britannia's true king. . . ."

†HE †VRΠIΠG

A·D· 515

It was the evening of Beltain, and the sun was with-drawing westward, trailing tattered standards of flame. From the Wall, Artor could see the flicker of bonfires here and there upon the land. *Like detachments that have been cut off from their main force and must stand alone against the dark—* A very mili-tary metaphor for the fires of spring, he thought grimly, but his heart was a battlefield, with no room for anything but war.

Some of the fires burned in the old fortress of Vercovicium, where his army had made camp. It was a central location, and until he knew whether Medraut meant to strike south-ward through Luguvalium or Dun Eidyn, as good a place as any to wait for news.

Here, the Wall took advantage of natural escarpments, with a view of the open country to either side. The water of the loughs reflected the sky's conflagration in fragments of flame. There were fires there as well, where the folk of scattered farmsteads had gathered to celebrate the festival.

On this night, no army would move. In the fort, his men could safely drink as much of the local beer as they had been able to collect on their march northward, but liquor would not drown Artor's sorrows. Instead he had set out to walk the Wall.

It curved away to the eastward, climbing the escarpments and swooping through the dales, even now, when parts of it were crumbling, a mighty testament to the empire it had defended. As he walked, the king fingered a fragment of bronze he had found among the stones, an old military badge with the image of an eagle, wishing it had the power to call to his aid the spirits of the men who had set these stones, as the image of the goddess had raised the ghosts at Mons Badonicus.

He had done what he could to pacify the land behind him, swearing new oaths with the sons of King Icel, and fighting a series of swift and bloody conflicts with the rebel lords of Demetia and Pagus and Guenet. They were a flock of fighting cocks, each crowing on his own dunghill. How quickly they had forgotten the host of enemies that waited beyond the farmyard wall!

This Wall, he thought, as his footfalls rang against the solid masonry. He peered into the shadow that was creeping across the northern lands. There lay the darkness that would extinguish the light of Britannia, where Medraut was gathering the wild tribes of the North. Their last defense was this slender line of stone.

Ahead, indeed, a section had fallen. Carefully, Artor clambered downward until he stood on the springy turf. The slope fell away before him, rising again to a pair of outcrops in stark silhouette against the fading sky. In the cleft between them he saw the sudden spark of a fire and started towards it.

Any one of his men who ventured thus into hostile territory, without orders and unsupported, would have been mucking out stables for a week, but Cai and Gualchmai were no longer here to scold him. Silent through the dusk, the king made his way forward, summoning all the woodcraft Merlin had taught him to move unseen. And in truth he did not think it was an enemy, but some sheepherd who would not grudge a stranger the warmth of his Beltain fire.

That flame, burning in the lee of a sandstone boulder, was the only light remaining in a darkening world. Artor closed his cloak to hide his mail and stepped towards it, wondering what they could be burning to make the air smell so sweet, as if the open moorland had somehow gathered all the rich scents of a woodland spring. He blinked at shadows laced with whirling sparkles of brightness that fled away at his approach until there was only one shape by the fire. As he drew nearer it straightened, light shining on a tangle of golden hair and glowing on the folds of a cloak striped and chequered in spring green.

Guendivar. . . .

Artor stopped short, staring. *A vision,* he thought numbly, *born of my need.* But no image in his memory matched this face that was both older than he remembered and as fresh as the hawthorne flowers that wreathed her brow. Would a vision have mud clinging to the hem of her tunica and leaves caught in her hair?

She is real! He could not even imagine how she came to be here. A flash of heat and chill together pebbled his skin.

"I bring a Beltain blessing from Britannia to her king. . . ." Her voice trembled as if the anxieties of humanity warred with the magic that still starred her eyes. He swallowed, remembering what reason she had to be afraid.

"What right have you to give such a blessing, who have betrayed both Britannia and me?"

Her cheeks grew first red, then pale, but her voice was steady as she replied. "The right of a priestess of Brigantia, whose land this is. I have not betrayed *her,* and what I give I have the right to take away."

"You have taken away my heart, and given another my bed and my throne!" Artor said bitterly, setting his hand on the hilt of his sword. "I should slay you where you stand!"

"Not your bed," she said in a low voice, "empty though it has been. The blade you bear is a Sword of Justice, which would refuse to touch me. You would do better to ask what gifts I bestow."

He let go of the pommel as if stung. His bed had been barren indeed, he thought in shame, but his soul was singing at the knowledge that Medraut had not lain with her there.

"What are your gifts . . . Lady?" The words limped from his lips.

"Sovereignty. Potency. Power."

Artor believed her. She had never been so beautiful arrayed in silk and gold as she was now, standing by the fire in her smudged gown. And in that moment he knew himself an empty husk, unfit to serve her.

"Guendivar. . . ." The anger that had strengthened his voice drained away. Throughout this war that fury had sustained him. He had nothing, now. "I have tried to hate you," he said tiredly, "but whatever you have done, it was my sin and my failure that was the cause. Can you believe that little though I showed it, you have always had my love?"

"My dear—" she said with a tenderness that pierced his heart. "I have had your letters. Do you think I did not know? But you did not come, and I grew heartsick and confused, and did what I thought I must for the sake of the land. If there is blame, much of it must be mine."

He stood before her with bowed head and empty hands. "I have lived by the sword for forty years, Guendivar, and I am tired. My peace is broken, and my people tear at each other like wolves. I have nothing left to give. . . ."

"Did I not say it?" she said softly. "The gifts are mine. I am the Tiernissa, the Queen. Come to me. . . ."

Step by unsteady step, he made his way around the fire. She reached up to unclasp the penannular brooch that pinned his cloak and began to unbuckle the belt that held his sword. He stopped her, glancing around him, calculating the distance back to the Wall.

"We are warded by sentinels more vigilant than any of your soldiers," said Guendivar. "Take off your armor, Artor, and perhaps you will be able to see. . . ."

Piece by piece the king laid his garments aside, until he stood defenseless in that place where faith is the companion of despair. It did not matter whether he believed her. Love or death would be equally welcome, if they came in her arms. The queen had also thrown down her green mantle and unpinned the fibulae that held her gown, so that she stood dressed only in her hawthorne crown.

"Thus do I salute you, for you are the head of the people—"
She stretched to kiss his brow.

Behind his closed eyes light flared, illuminating past and present so that he saw and understood the meanings and connections between all things.

Her hands moved down his shoulders and the blossoms of her crown brushed soft against his breast as her lips pressed the skin above his heart. "I salute you, for you are the protector of the nation—"

At the words, fire filled his breast, and a purifying protective tenderness that would dare all dangers, not from hatred, but for love.

Then Guendivar bent to his thighs, her fingers sliding softly along the track left by Melwas' spear. He drew in a sharp breath as her lips touched his phallus and he felt it rise.

"I salute you, for you are the Lord of the Land—"

Artor clutched at her shoulders, shaken by the raw pulse of power that leaped from the earth to flare through every limb, his stiffened member straining against her hand.

She tipped her head back, gazing up at him. "Oh my beloved, come to me!"

No man living could have resisted that command. The queen drew him down beside the stone, her white thighs opening to enfold him, and in her arms the power that filled him found its rightful outlet at last.

Conquered and conqueror, giving and receiving, very swiftly Artor ceased to distinguish between Guendivar's ecstasy and his own. And in the ultimate moment, when the entire essence of being was focused to a single point, even that blossomed in an expansion of awareness that included himself and Guendivar and the earth beneath them and all the hallowed isle.

Afterward, he and Guendivar lay beside the fire, wrapped in their cloaks against the chill they had not felt before. When her head rested thus, upon his shoulder, Artor knew there could be no wrong anywhere. If he had not been filled with joy, he could have wept for all the nights when they had lain separate in the royal bed.

"If we had a ship we could sail away to the Blessed Isles," he murmured against her hair.

She shook her head a little, nestling closer. "I think we have run far enough, you and I. It is we who must bring a blessing to *this* Isle."

"As you have given it to me. . . ." Artor smiled. "But what power brought you to me here?"

"Merlin took me from Medraut's fort. God knows what tales they will be telling—they must think that Ninive and I vanished into the air!" Her laughter faded as she told the tale. "But it was the fair folk who brought me to this place, though I hardly expected the High King of Britannia to be wandering alone on the moor."

"Not quite alone. There are something over four thousand men camped in the old fort—" He gestured towards the irregular line of the Wall, dark against the stars. "I had meant to pursue Medraut all the way to Fodreu, but now I do not know what I should do."

"Stay here," answered Guendivar, "where you have a source of supply and some protection. Medraut is raising the North against you—better to meet him on your own home ground." She began to speak of what she had learned during her captivity concerning the strength of the enemy and Medraut's plans.

"I suppose we should get up," he said finally. "My men will be wondering what has become of *me*."

"Need we go back quite yet?" Guendivar laughed a little, reaching up to kiss his ear.

To his delight, Artor's body responded—he had wondered if their loving would be a reproduceable miracle. He kissed her, and matters proceeded from there, and this time, if their joining did not quite reach the earlier excesses of ecstasy, he was better able to appreciate the solid reality of the woman in his arms.

Merlin sat with eyes half-closed and his back against an oak tree, listening to his heart drum in his breast. Nearby, Ninive was building up the fire and preparing a framework of willow twigs to cook the string of trout she had caught in the stream. From time to time she would glance at him, frowning, but she had said no word.

She's afraid to ask . . . he thought grimly. *Well, that's no wonder.* What had begun as a shortness of breath on the journey through Pictland had become a general weakness, as if with every step the life within him was bleeding back into the soil. Three weeks had passed since Beltain, and they had scarcely gone the distance he used to run in a day.

He himself did not feel fear so much as amazement that the body which had endured so many years past the normal span of men was failing at last. *It could have chosen a better moment to go,* he thought then. But most men, he had heard, found themselves unready when their time came at last.

He had rescued Guendivar, and the faerie folk told him she was reunited with the king. Indeed, he had hardly needed telling, for the joy of their reunion had reverberated through the land. But the spirits spoke also of a mighty hosting in the land of the Pretani. He had dreamed of a fort above a river, where men fought and died. Soon, Artor would face his greatest battle, and Merlin would not be there.

When he closed his eyes, he saw the face of the daimon of his prophecies, wide-eyed with wisdom and ethereally fair. When he opened them, he saw Ninive, as bright of hair, but with fine skin browned by sun and wind, and anxiety clouding her dark eyes. She had gone back entirely to the dress of her mother's people, a woolen skirt whose ragged fringe brushed her knees, and a skin cape pinned at the breast by a sharpened bone. Barefoot, she could fade into the woods like one of the folk of faerie. She knew the wildlands as he did, the perfect companion for his wanderings, but could she become something more?

"My lord, the fish is cooked—see how the flesh flakes off the bones." Ninive knelt beside him, offering the trout on a dock leaf.

"I will try." He smiled. He picked up fragments of the trout with a delicate touch.

"I am thinking," said Ninive when they were done, "that if I were to leave food here for you, I could fetch help and bring you to some farmstead where you could rest. . . ."

He shook his head. "We have to go on."

"Not all the way to the Wall!" she protested. "It would be harvest before we arrived, and you—" She broke off, looking away.

"Will likely not get there," he finished for her. "Do you think I do not know?" The face she turned to him was anguished, and he stretched out a hand already thinner than it had been a week ago. "My little one, do you care so much for me?"

Ninive gestured around her. "You have given me back my soul!" She took his hand and pressed her forehead against it. With his other hand, very gently, he touched her hair.

"I am ninety years old and had begun to fear myself immortal. In truth, I am relieved to find it is not so. In the forest, when a creature grows too weak to hunt food, death comes soon. I would tell you to leave me here—"

"I would not do it!" she interrupted.

"But I must ask something harder. Great forces are gathering against the king, and I cannot be there. I have dreamed of a future that fills me with fear. I must use the time that is left to me so that something will survive."

She stared at him, her eyes dark as forest pools. "What do you need me to do?"

"There is a place that I must find before Midsummer Day. It lies deep in the Forest of Caledon—" He gestured southward. "When we reach it, we will work a mighty magic."

Beltain, or perhaps the queen, had brought in the summer. Even along the Wall, flowers bloomed and grass grew tall, and on the moors the heather, weighted with an emperor's wealth of purple bloom, hummed with the song of bees. Now the days lengthened rapidly towards midsummer's epiphany.

Artor made good use of the time. New messages had gone out across Britannia, proclaiming that king and queen were once more united, and calling the warriors to a great hosting at Vercovicium. At this season the demands of the fields kept many on their farmsteads, but each day, it seemed, another group of riders would come jogging along the Military Way that ran below the Wall.

"You see, they are still loyal," said Guendivar, gazing down from the walkway of the fortress wall at the moving tapestry of men and horses below.

"It is your name that has brought them," Artor replied, putting his arms around her. "They know that the sovereignty of Britannia is returned to me."

She leaned against him, the warmth of his touch still filling her with wonder. It was now well into June, and the weather had turned bright and fair; the long northern dusk spread a veil of amethyst across the hills. In the evening peace, sounds carried clearly.

"What is that?" she asked, as a noise like distant thunder began to overwhelm the ordinary sounds of the camp below.

She felt Artor stiffen. He lifted his hand to shade his eyes from the westering sun, staring at the Military Way, where something was moving, dust boiling behind it in a plume. She turned to look up at him. Already the hard stare of the commander was replacing the tenderness in his eyes.

"A messenger," he said grimly, "who rides at too headlong a pace to bear good news."

Medraut had taken Luguvalium. The chieftains of the Selgovae, still resenting the taxes Artor had laid upon them a dozen years ago, had joined him in a swift drive southward, and Morcant Bulc of Dun Breatann, denying his father's treaties, had joined them. The main body of the Picts had not yet appeared, but their most likely route would be eastward through the Votadini lands. Artor had been aware of the danger, and ordered Cunobelinus to stay where he was and defend Dun Eidyn. But if Medraut held one end of the Wall and the Picts the other, the king's force would be caught in between.

The solution, obviously, was to attack Medraut first and destroy him. Artor got his men to Luguvalium in two days of hard marching and was preparing to attack the fort by the time Guendivar, following more slowly, caught up with him.

The wind carried a faint reek of something burning, and the air resounded with the yammering of crows. Guendivar gazed up at her husband, searching for words with which to say good-bye.

All her life, she had heard stories of Artor's battles, but she had never before seen him armed for war. The gilded scales of his hauberk gleamed in the sunlight and his mantle was of the purple of emperors. The big black horse stamped and snorted as he reined it in outside the little church at the edge of the town where he had taken her.

"Stay here, my heart—" he said, leaning down to touch her hair. "If we destroy them here, I will come for you, but if they flee, we will be pursuing, and you will be safer behind us." His shield was new, but the horse's harness and Artor's leather leg wrappings and the heavy wool tunic showed signs of hard wear.

"But how will I know—"

"If we win, I daresay someone will tell you." He laughed, his teeth flashing in the close-cropped beard. It was threaded with silver, but his hair still grew strongly. Her hands clenched as she fought the desire to bury her fingers in its thick waves once more.

"And if we lose—" His face sobered. "You must stay hidden and make your way south somehow. Do not fail me, my lady, for if I fall, only you can pass on the sovereignty."

"Do not say it!" she exclaimed. "I will not lose you now!"

"Guendivar . . . I will always be with you. . . ."

Behind him a horn blared and the king straightened, sliding the helmet he had carried in the crook of his arm onto his head. With nasal and side-flanges covering most of his face, he was suddenly a stranger. The stallion reared and Artor reined it around. The men of his escort fell in behind him, and then they were away.

The queen stared after them, and only when the echo of hoofbeats on cobblestones had faded did she allow the tears to come.

All through that endless day she prayed, kneeling on the worn planking of the church's floor, though she hardly knew which god it was to whom she addressed her prayers. About the middle of the afternoon, she heard a great clamor that gradually diminished until there were only a few dogs barking, and then, one by one, the voices of the people of the town.

Presently the old priest who served the church came back again.

"The king is safe, or at least he was an hour ago. But the Perjurer broke through his lines and fled with most of his men, and our army has gone after him, save for a detachment left under Prince Peretur to guard you and the town. Let us praise the Lord of Hosts, who gives victory!"

At night the Forest of Caledon was full of whispers; the wind continuing its conversation with the trees. Merlin felt the vibration through the trunk behind him, just as it thrummed through the shaft of the Spear at his side. Sitting so, his thoughts matched themselves to the long slow rhythms of the forest, and the rustle of leaf and twig became the words of a dialogue between the Goddess who lived in the earth and the God.

As the journey continued, the Druid understood them ever more clearly. By day he clung to the pony Ninive had brought for him, riding by balance. At night, when the girl lay breathing softly by the embers of their fire, Merlin became a tree, drawing from soil and sky the energy he needed to go on. But the earth drummed with distant hoofbeats and the wind rang with the crying of ravens, calling their kindred to a great killing, and he dared not succumb to the forest's peace.

And each day the hours of twilight lengthened as the season turned towards the solstice, all powers drawing together to resolve the conflict that had unbalanced the land.

At the Isle of Maidens, Morgause woke from evil dreams. It lacked a week to midsummer, and the priestesses were preparing for the festival, but her nightmares had been filled with blood and battle. She saw Artor and Medraut facing each other in battered armor, fury stamping their faces with its own likeness, and felt the perspiration break out on her brow. In that confrontation she sensed some great turning of fate, and it filled her with fear.

She left her chamber, calling to her maidens. "Pack journey food and blankets. Nest and Verica, you will come with me."

"But Lady," they protested, "what about the sacred rites, the festival?"

"This year the Lady of Ravens is celebrating her own ritual," she said heavily. "I must be at the Wall by Midsummer Day. . . ."

"Midsummer Eve . . ." said Goriat, surveying the winding river and the bluff above it, where lights twinkled from the old fortress. "At home, the clans will be gathering to light their solstice fires, throwing flaming brands high into the air to make the crops grow, and carrying the torches through the fields."

"In the South, also," answered Artor.

He felt as if he were thinking with two minds, one part evaluating the site's military potential while the other appreciated the beauty of the scene. The fort stood on a crag with a steep escarpment. Below stretched flats through which a small river wound. The higher ground was astir with men and horses as the Britons settled in.

"How strange that this stream should also have the name of Cam," the younger man said then.

The king shrugged. "Britannia is full of rivers that turn and wind in their courses, and I suppose many of them must bear that name." He walked along the riverbank, his officers following.

"You must wish it was the one that runs near Camalot."

"Only if I were inside its walls," Artor answered with grim humor. "If I must attack a fortress, I am glad it is not a place of my own building. Camboglanna was strong once, but now it is in disrepair, and Medraut is not provisioned for a seige."

"He has trapped himself, then—" Goriat grinned.

Vortipor shook his head. "Not if the Picts arrive to relieve him. That's our danger. He can't outrun us, so he hopes to outwait us—"

"—Until he outnumbers us. I see." Goriat squinted up at the fort. "The old Romans built well. To see that ragtag of northerners occupying Camboglanna galls my soul! An attack uphill from this side would be difficult, and I don't suppose the far side is any better."

Peretur shrugged. "The Wall joins the edge of the fort on both sides and there is only one gate, still in good repair."

Goriat turned to Artor. "We'll have to winkle him out of there somehow, my lord."

Artor's gaze was still on the river—the gleam of late sunlight on the water shone like Guendivar's hair. *I have been fighting too long.* He sighed. *I want to take her with me somewhere they have never heard of warfare—perhaps the Blessed Isles.* But he had to fight one more battle. If he could win that one perhaps he would be done.

"I'll send a message. Medraut has run from me twice now. If force won't budge him, we'll see what shame will do."

They gazed up at the road that crossed the overgrown vallum ditch before the walls. Dark figures moved on the walkway above it, bows in their hands.

"I'll deliver it," said Goriat with a sigh. "We were brothers once. He might hesitate before ordering those archers to shoot me. . . ."

Above Camboglanna, two ravens circled, then swung out over the river and settled, calling, in the branches of a gnarled thorn tree.

Raven wings filled Merlin's vision with fragments of shadow. He clung to the saddle bow, drawing breath harshly, willing the wheeling world to slow. Over the tumult in his head he heard someone calling him—

"My lord, I have found the spring!"

He opened his eyes and found Ninive, a fixed point around which the world stilled to comprehensible shape and meaning. The ravens were at Camboglanna. Here, there were only the irregular flitterings of wren and tit, and the musical gurgle of a tiny stream.

Before him, the narrow leaves of young rowan trees moved gently in the breeze, their edges gilded by the westering sun. Below spread a hawthorne to whose twigs a few fading white blossoms still clung. Beyond them he saw a noble oak tree.

"The water flows from that outcrop of rock just beyond the

trees—" Ninive danced back across the jumble of fallen leaves and mossy boulders. Through the tangle of branches loomed the side of the hill.

"It is the place. . . . The headwaters of the Cam," he muttered, nodding as he recognized each feature of the image that had haunted his dreams. "And the day—have we come too late? Tell me, what is the day?"

"By the calculations you gave me at the beginning of this journey, this will be the shortest night of the year," she replied.

He sat back with a long sigh. "Midsummer Eve. They will fight tomorrow by the river."

"Can you help?" asked the girl. "Will the water carry your power to Artor?"

"Can anyone turn fate?" he murmured. "Now, at least, I have a chance to try!"

He slid from the pony's back, and with Ninive and the Spear to prop him, made his way to the oak, whose knobbed root made a seat above the stream. There he sat, extending his senses to encompass every part of the wood around him, and waited, as at Camboglanna two armies were waiting, for the dawning of the longest day.

The first sunlight gleamed from the river and from the helmets of the men who stood beside it: Artor's army, in full battle array. Medraut could see them clearly. So could his men. They were talking about the damned letter. Did they think he could not hear?

He had burned the parchment, but the words were burned in his memory.

"You boast of your courage, but twice now you have run from my wrath. You boast of your right to rule, but the queen has fled you and returned to my bed. . . ."

Guendivar! Oh, Artor had known that would enrage him. In dreams he still held her rounded body in his arms.

The hateful words echoed in his inner ear—his mother's scolding voice, speaking his father's words.

"Like a greedy child, you have tried to seize your inheritance,

*and by doing so, forfeited all claim! You are coward and craven—
tainted in blood and corrupt in mind."*

And if I am, Mother, he thought in bitter reply, *I am what
you and he have made me!* And still the accusations rolled on.

*"And these things all men shall know for truth if you do not
come out and face me, body to body and soul to soul!"*

Ravens were circling in the air below, calling out to their
goddess the tally of the slain. He had only to wait, Medraut
thought furiously, and they would all be safe. But these
bloodthirsty fools whom he commanded were chafing to
avenge their defeat at Luguvalium.

"My lord," said Bleitisbluth, "the men are angry. The enemy have been shouting evil things. The Rome-king left a
garrison in Luguvalium, and we outnumber them. Better to
order our warriors to attack while you still can!"

The raven voices grew louder, blended to a single voice,
calling to him. *Guendivar is lost to me,* he thought, *I must serve
the Lady of Ravens now. . . .*

"Very well—if they are so eager for battle, fight they shall!"
Certainty came to Medraut like a spark kindling tinder, and
with it a fierce exultation. He reeled off a list of chieftains,
their order and numbers. "The remainder will form a reserve
force, hidden here, with me."

Medraut watched from the gatehouse as his army rolled
down to meet the waiting force below. The men of the North
rode their sturdy ponies to battle, but they fought on foot,
with shield and spear. The narrow flats by the river favored
them. He had expected that Artor would not be able to use
his cavalry to full advantage, and indeed, he could see that
the king himself was fighting dismounted.

As the morning passed, the purple cloak was everywhere
on the field, the pendragon floating above it as Artor's standard bearer strove to keep up with him. As noon drew nearer,
the sun's strength grew.

He is an old man, thought Medraut, *and it's getting hotter.
Soon, he will fail!*

From below came clouds of dust, stopping the throat and
stinging the eyes. The only color was the crimson of blood,

bright as the cloak of the goddess of battles in the pitiless radiance of Midsummer Day.

What kept Merlin upright was the Spear. He had taken his stand in the space between the oak, the mountain ash trees, and the thorn, just where the waters of the Cam emerged from the stone. His heart galloped like Artor's warhorse, vision pulsing in time to its beat. Increasingly he relied on inner senses, extending them through air and soil until his body no longer contained his awareness. He risked losing focus entirely, but his control would last long enough, he thought, for what he had to do.

"Cast the circle, Ninive—"

The girl's voice rose and fell as she paced sunwise around him, sprinkling the sacred herbs, chanting in the old tongue of her mother's people. She was weeping, but her voice stayed strong, and he had time for a moment of pride. Nine times she made the circuit, and with each circumnambulation the Druid's consciousness drew inward, trading the diffuse awareness of his earlier state for a more powerful and precise connection with the space immediately around him, as if he stood within a pillar of crystal bounded by oak and ash and thorn.

Then she completed the spell, and he needed his control no longer, for the magic upheld him. Ninive was a spark of light before him, sensed rather than seen.

"The hour moves towards the triumph of the sun, the longest day! I summon you, O Prophet of Britannia, to say what shall come to this land."

For a moment Merlin knew nothing. Then the daimon within him awakened and his mind reeled beneath the flood of foreknowledge.

"The Red Dragon gives birth to a Boar and a litter of little Foxes that between them shall tear and worry at the land. Men and women shall cry out and flee their rulers, and give their name to Armorica, for it is the princes of their own people that oppress them. And then the White Dragon shall rise from his sleep and devour them, from Land's End to the Orcades."

Immensities of time and space rushed before him; he saw strange armies marching across Britannia, steel roads and devastated forests and cities covering the land. He saw a crossed banner that circled the world. The images he saw he could not comprehend, and presently he waited in silence once more.

"When these things come to pass, O Prophet, where will you be?" A new question came.

"I will be Lailoken in the court of Gwendoleu, and in the court of Urien I will be Taliessin. I shall not leave this land, but ever and again I will shape myself as her need compels me. Going in and out of the body, my voice will be heard in Britannia throughout the ages." In vision, all those lives were clear before him, and Merlin laughed.

"The sun nears her nooning, master, and there is one thing more to ask. Say now what fate is twined for Artor the king!"

The vision that had spanned centuries folded cataclysmically inward, arrowing like lightning towards its goal. Merlin saw the bloody field of Camboglanna, and Artor, catching his breath as he leaned upon a broken spear. Goriat lay dead beside him, but his enemies were fleeing up the hill. Above them the God of the Sword and the Lady of Ravens hovered, invisible to mortal eyes. And then the air rang with the bitter music of warpipes, and from the fortress a troop of mounted men came riding, and Medraut sped before them.

The bean-sidhe *is wailing-* thought Artor, *that doom-singing demon that Cunorix used to speak of so long ago.* He wiped sweat from his eyes with the back of his hand and peered up at the fort, knowing already that it was something worse. The army he had faced was gone, but Medraut, whom he had sought in vain all through the battle, was coming out at last. *Now,* he thought despairingly, *when I am already tired.* But this was no time to stand swearing.

"Edrit, run—tell Vortipor to get ready!" he called to the warrior who bore his standard, and started to slog back to the high ground. Medraut had been clever to field a reserve force when the battle was almost done. But Artor had been clever too.

He heard a gleeful shout as the enemy sighted him, and struggled towards the line of willow trees.

On the other side, Vortipor waited with the best riders the British had. A boy was holding Artor's big black stallion, a descendent of the first Raven he had ridden to war. Edrit boosted him into the saddle and handed him a javelin and a horseman's round shield. Taking up the reins, he peered through the screen of branches. Medraut's troop had reached the bottom of the hill. They were losing speed as they spread out along the road.

He turned back to his men. "Has it been hot here, waiting? It was hot work down there too! But now it's your turn, my lads, and you are the veterans of Gallia. Keep your formation, and that rabble will scatter like bees from an overturned hive!"

Someone murmured, "But they can still sting!" And the others laughed.

They started forward, Vortipor taking the point and Artor riding among the men on the wing. As the rebels turned towards the river, the king's men burst through the willows, urging their mounts to full gallop as the slope lent them momentum.

"Artor!" cried the British riders. "Artor and Britannia!"

They were going to hit the enemy at an angle. The king wrapped his long legs around Raven's sides, dropped the knotted reins on the horse's neck, and cocked his arm, poising the javelin to throw.

He sighted on Medraut, then the point of the British wedge struck, and Artor was carried past him. Training ingrained to the point of instinct selected a new target; he cast, and a man fell. A spearpoint drove towards him; he lifted his shield and grunted as it took the weight of the weapon, shifted his weight and jerked as the horse moved, and felt the spear tear from the man's grip and clatter to the ground.

He thrust the shield outward to protect his body as he reached across his belly to grip the hilt of the Chalybe sword. *May the Defender be with me!* he prayed, and felt a tremor of eagerness shock through his hand. At the battle of Verulamium the god of the Sword had come himself to counter an alien magic, but this was a battle of men, and Artor dared ask only for the strength to endure to the end.

The black horse was fresh and knew its trade, wheeling to knock a smaller beast sideways so that Artor could finish the rider with a slash of his sword. Then another shape loomed up before him. He struck, and struck again. The sweat ran hot beneath his armor, for the sun stood high. After each blow his arm came back up more slowly, yet still he slew, seeing Medraut's mocking face on every foe.

The sun stood high, and all the wood trembled beneath the weight of its glory. The circle of power where Merlin stood was a dazzle of light. But his inner sight was filled with the image of Artor, fighting on while all around him men fled or fell.

An enemy sword cracked the king's shield; Merlin saw him lose his balance and tumble from the horse's back. In the next moment his opponent was downed by a thrown javelin. Artor struggled to his knees at the water's edge, shieldless, but still clinging to his sword. The king looked up. Medraut stood before him.

Merlin gripped the shaft of the Spear. "Is it time?" he whispered, and the rune-carved wood quivered like a live thing in his hand. In all the forest, there was no sound but the sweet music of the infant stream. "This is my will," he said aloud, "that my spirit shall neither sleep nor seek the Summerland, but continue to wander the world!

"I am the wind on the wave!" Merlin cried.

"I am the fire in the wood!

"I am the sun beneath the sea and the seed in the stone.

"Before time's beginning I was with the gods, and I will sing at its end.

"I am Wild Man and Witega, Druid and daimon—

"I invoke the land of Britannia to the aid of her king!"

The Spear whirled in his hand, and he plunged it, point downward, into the moist soil. Deep, deep it sank, to the roots of creation, but the wooden shaft was expanding, extending branches to embrace the sky. For an eternal moment, Merlin was the Tree, linking earth and heaven.

Then the world collapsed around him in a roar of falling stone. But the essence that had been Merlin was already shaping itself to root and branch, to soil and stone and the rising wind, but most powerfully to the winding waters at his feet. Swift as thought he sped southward towards Camboglanna.

RAVEN OF THE SUN

A.D. 515

MEDRAUT WAS A FACELESS SHADOW BETWEEN ARTOR AND the sun.

"So, my lord father, you kneel before me! Will you admit you are beaten at last?"

The king squinted up at him, licking blood from a lip that had split when he hit the ground. His helmet had come off; the air felt cool on his sweat-soaked hair. It was a little past noon.

"I kneel to the earth, whose power brought me down," he said evenly. "Are you going to let me get up, or do I have to fight you from my knees?" They were getting wet; he looked down and realized that he had fallen in the shallows at the edge of the stream.

Medraut slowly lifted his sword. *He's tired*, Artor observed, but he himself was exhausted. Perhaps it would be easier to fight from here. Or to let Medraut kill him. They were surrounded by the dead and dying. He had lost his army, he thought numbly, and Britannia.

The river ran purling past his foot, sweet and clear. When Medraut still did not answer, the king scooped up a handful of water.

His first thought was that he had not known he was so thirsty. He dipped up more, and felt his tissues expanding like parched earth in the rain. With the third mouthful, he sensed the triumphant surge of Merlin's spirit making him one with everything around him. The cool sweetness of water, the solid strength of earth, the dry heat of the air—he felt them all with an intensity that was almost pain.

A movement that would have been impossible a moment before brought the king to his feet. Medraut jumped back, staring.

"Thank you . . ." Artor whispered, but it was not his opponent to whom he was speaking. He swayed, and Medraut started forward, sword swinging high.

A smooth twist brought the king on guard, bringing up the Sword of the Defender two-handed to deflect Medraut's blow. The clangor as the two blades met echoed across the vale. Artor's knees bent slightly, the great sword drifting up to hover above his right shoulder.

"Why did you do this, Medraut? Why did you try to destroy Britannia?"

His son looked at him uncomprehending. "I wanted to rule—"

Artor shook his head. "The land cannot be ruled, only served."

Medraut's mouth twisted and he lunged. "You left her! You left *me!*"

For a moment the king hesitated, the truth of that accusation piercing more deeply than any enemy sword. Then strength surged up from the soil once more and he knew that he was still the Lady's Champion.

Artor leaped back, sword sweeping down and to the side, knocking his son's weapon away and spinning him so that for a moment they stood with shoulders touching, as if they met in the dance.

"I was promised everything, and then betrayed," hissed Medraut. "I came to you, since my mother had cast me aside like a tool she no longer wanted to use. And you banished me to the barbarians and *forgot* me! I've had to fight for my life, my name. . . ." He whirled away, the rest hanging unspoken between them—*for Guendivar. . . .*

"Surrender and you shall rule the North," said Artor, his breath coming fast.

"I could win it all yet, *Father.* . . ." Medraut advanced with a series of flashing blows that kept the king busy defending.

"Not while I live!" Artor knocked the younger man's last stroke aside with a force that sent him reeling.

"You will die, at my hand, or the hand of time—" answered Medraut, panting. "The heirs of Britannia are young foxes, eager to gnaw out their own little kingdoms, and that will be the end of your dream."

Instinctively Artor settled to guard, but his mind was whirling. He bore the Sword of the Defender, but what could a dead man defend? He looked up at the mocking face of his son. Men called Medraut the Perjurer, but surely Deceiver would be a better name, sent to tempt him to despair. And yet the power of that impossible moment of connection with the land still sang in his veins.

"Oh Medraut, is there room for nothing in your heart but hate?"

"You took the only thing I might have loved!" Medraut cried out in answer, and ran at him with wildly swinging sword.

Artor retreated, using all his skill to fend that blade away. The boy was a good swordsman, but he was battering with berserker fury as if he meant to obliterate, not merely kill. Forty years of experience kept the king's weapon between him and that deadly blade. It was those same battle-trained reflexes, not Artor's will, that halted Medraut's charge at last with a stop-thrust that pierced through hauberk and breastbone and out the other side.

For a moment they stared into each other's eyes. Then Medraut's features contorted. His weapon slipped from his hand, and Artor felt the weight of the boy's body begin to drag down the sword. He stepped back, and the blade slid free as Medraut fell, the bright blood—his son's blood—staining the steel.

The air rang with silence.

"Father...." A little blood was running from Medraut's mouth. The king knelt beside him, laying down the Chalybe sword, reaching to ease off his son's helm and smooth back the hair from his brow as if he had been a little child. Medraut's eyes widened, meeting his father's gaze unbarriered at last, shock transmuting gradually into an appalled understanding.

Then he twisted, hand clutching at his side. "It is not *my* blood," he whispered, "that will consecrate the ground—"

He convulsed once more, thrusting the dagger that had been sheathed at his hip up beneath Artor's mail. It seared along the old scar where Melwas had wounded the king long ago and stabbed upward into his groin.

For a moment all other awareness disappeared in a red wave of agony. When it began to recede, Artor looked down and saw that Medraut lay still and sightless, his face upturned to the sun.

Oh, Lady— thought the king, *is this your sacrifice?*

He could feel the warm seep of blood across his thigh and the beginnings of a deeper agony. Slowly he lowered himself to the earth beside the body of his son, vision flashing dark and bright with each pulse, fixing on the pebble that lay beside him. A glowing spiral spun within the stone. Artor's fingers closed upon its solid certainty.

This is the king stone ... the heart of Britannia. It was beneath my feet all along.

His hearing must be going too, he thought then, for his head rang with strange music ... like Gaulish battle horns. ...

Guendivar gasped and reached out to Peretur for support as pain stabbed upward through her womb.

"My lady, what is it? Are you ill?"

She tried to straighten, staring round at the men who had come with her to the marketplace. Blood and dust and sunlight filled her vision; she saw an old fortress on a hill.

"Camboglanna..." she whispered. "Artor has been wounded!"

As the words articulated her inner vision, she was aware

of a great surge of mingled grief and exultation that seemed to rise from the very soil.

"Lady, the king told us to guard you here!" said Peretur in alarm.

She shook her head. "The battle is over. If you want to keep me safe, then follow, for go to him I will!" She started towards the stables, and after a moment the men came after her.

To Morgause, the moment was like a shadow on the sun, a shudder in the soil. She stood swaying in the road, suddenly finding it hard to breathe. Luguvalium lay a day and a half behind them. To left and right rose the outriders of the moors. Ahead, the Wall marched over the first of the crags, and brown dust stained the sky.

"What is it?" cried her priestesses. "What do you hear?"

"I hear a calling of ravens," whispered Morgause, "I hear the groans of dying men. The blood of kings soaks into the soil. We must go quickly, if we are to get there in time!"

"In time for what?" asked Nest, hurrying after her, but Morgause did not reply.

Ninive stood weeping before the tumble of earth and stone where once a cliff had been. Oak and ash and thorn had disappeared beneath the landslip, and with them all trace of the Druid who had used her aid to perform his last and greatest act of magic, but from beneath the rubble, the little stream still trickled, singing to the stones.

Merlin had accomplished what he intended, but had he saved the king? She knew only that there had been a great shift in the fabric of reality. What would he want her to do? Ninive dried her tears and stood listening, and it seemed to her that in the whisper of the wind and the gurgle of the stream she heard his voice once more.

She picked up the bag in which she had carried their food, and began to follow the course of the Cam south, toward the Wall.

*   *   *

Consciousness returned slowly. Artor drew a very careful breath, wondering how long he had lain wounded for his body to have already begun to learn ways to avoid the pain. He could feel the wound as a dull ache in his lower belly, but his flesh held the memory of a throbbing agony.

People were talking in low voices nearby—someone must have survived. He must have wakened before, already fevered, for he had thought that Morgause was there, and Betiver. The king opened his eyes and blinked, recognizing a Roman hauberk and curling dark hair threaded with grey.

"My lord! You are with us again!" Betiver turned and knelt beside him, his fine features bronzed with campaigning and drawn with strain.

"And so are you," answered Artor. "Old friend, what are you doing here?" He had been unconscious for some time, he thought, for his wound had been bandaged, and he was lying inside some roughly repaired building in the fortress.

"We could get no news—" Betiver said helplessly. "I thought you might need me. I came as swiftly as I could—dear God, if only I had come in time!"

"You did." The king's gaze moved around the room, seeing only Betiver's men. "We won. . . ."

"The field was already yours when I got here," said Betiver. "My men have scoured it, seeking survivors. A few of the rebels got away. Vortipor is alive, though wounded, and a few others—pitifully few."

Artor drew a long sigh and winced as his belly began to ache again. "I saw Goriat fall . . ." he said.

Betiver nodded. "Morgause has gone out to look for him. We were grateful to have someone so skilled in leechcraft join us," he added with reluctant appreciation. "It was she who dressed your wound."

"My poor sister. She has lost all her sons . . ." said Artor. *And so have I*, he thought then, and the tide of grief that followed bore him once more down into the dark.

Once, as a child, she had been told the tale of Niobe, who had boasted too loudly of her children, and seen them taken by the gods. Now, thought Morgause as she searched the field of Camboglanna, she wept Niobe's tears.

The dead lay scattered like chaff in a newly reaped field; ravens stalked among them, gleaning their share of the grisly harvest. Selgovae and Saxons lay sprawled together, Dumnonians and Demetians, men from every corner of Britannia, in death there was no distinction between Medraut's rebels and those who had stayed loyal to Artor. This was not like the Saxon wars, when Britons had fought invaders from across the sea. There could be no winner in such a conflict as this had been, no matter which side claimed victory.

She had found Goriat early on. With him, she mourned Aggarban and Gwyhir and Gualchmai, but in a sense, she had lost them all a long time ago. The grief that kept her creeping from one body to another, turning them to peer at contorted faces, had been born when her youngest son left the Isle of Maidens, cursing her name.

That longest of days was beginning to draw to an end by the time she discovered Medraut. Betiver had said that his body had lain next to that of the king, but after Artor was taken up, the corpse must have been moved by the men who had served with the king in Gallia. It had not only been moved, she saw now, but hacked and slashed in posthumous vengeance so that without Betiver's description she would not have known which wound had been made by the Chalybe sword.

She carried water from the river and bathed the body as once she had bathed her child. They had stripped Medraut as well as mutilating him, but she could still see that her son had grown into a beautiful man—fair in body, at least, if not in soul. Cleansed of blood, his face bore a familiar sneering smile.

"And whose fault was that?" she muttered as she covered him with her veil. "Surely you were my most successful creation, a weapon aimed and sharpened which has finally struck home." He had pierced her to the heart as well.

"Is this all my doing?" Morgause gazed around her, shivering despite the warmth of the sun. "Ah, Medraut, even now I cannot hate you without hating myself as well!"

At the Isle of Maidens she had been kept too busy to think about the past; now it overwhelmed her. If she had had a blade, in that moment she might have executed her own self-judgment, but the fallen weapons had already been collected.

A raven fluttered to the ground nearby, its beak opening in a groan; in a moment two more followed it.

"You shall not have him!" Morgause exclaimed, and in their cries she heard an answer.

"I shall have all of them . . . from my bloody womb they are born, and in blood they return to me. Weep, my daughter, for all slain sons, and for all the mothers who will mourn them—weep with Me!"

The lamentations of the ravens rang around her, but the wail that rose from her belly to her breast to burst from her throat was far louder—a ullullation of mourning that echoed from the escarpment. Hearing it, men crossed themselves or flexed fingers in the sign of the Horns, looking over their shoulders.

But Morgause, when that cry had gone out of her, felt her own burden of grief a little lessened, knowing she did not mourn alone. Presently she heard the creak of wheels as men came with the cart to gather the corpses for the funeral pyre.

"Treat him with honor," Morgause said harshly, as they bent to take up Medraut's body, "for he came of the blood of kings."

"Lady, will you return to the fortress?" asked the troop leader. "They said that the king has awakened and is in pain."

The king . . . she thought numbly. Artor still needed her. She would have to live, at least for awhile.

"He is still alive?" Guendivar slid down from the horse and staggered as her muscles cramped from the long ride. Torchlight chased distorted shadows across the yard of the fortress. It was after midnight, but she had insisted they continue without stopping, desperate to reach Artor.

"The king lives," said Betiver, "but—"

She stumbled past him up the steps of the praetorium, where the roof had been repaired with rough thatching. An oil-lamp cast a fitful light on the sleeping man and the woman who sat by him. At Guendivar's step, she rose, and the queen stiffened, recognizing in the drawn features a reflection of Medraut.

Morgause stepped back abruptly, as if she had seen that moment of recoil. "You will wish to be with him. There is no more I can do for now." With a rustle of draperies she left the room.

The queen sank down upon the bench and took Artor's hand. It was warm, as if within, the solstice fires still burned. She laid her own fingers, chilled by her ride, upon his brow, and saw the flickers of pain that moved beneath his dreaming fade, and the firm lips within the curling beard curve in a little smile.

Presently his eyes opened. "I dreamed I was in Demetia . . . the Irish campaign. But you are here. . . ."

Guendivar nodded. She had been with him in Demetia too, but not like this, her soul seeking his like a homing bird.

"And I am here"— Artor grimaced —"for awhile. . . ." She started to protest, but he shook his head. "I always expected to die in battle, but I had hoped for a clean kill."

"It is only the wound fever," she said desperately. "We healed you before!"

"Well, we shall see. . . ." His voice trailed off. "God knows, now that we are together at last, I want. . . ." His eyes closed. She bent over him in panic, but it was only sleep.

She set her arms about him, calling on the goddess who had filled her at Beltain, and presently there came to her, not the exultant sexual power that had awakened the king's manhood, but a brooding, maternal tenderness—Brigantia, comforting her fallen champion, her most beloved child.

Through the remaining hours of darkness, a little longer than the night before, Guendivar dozed, cradling her king in her arms. When the light of morning began to filter through the thatching, she heard voices outside and, looking up, saw Ninive. As the young woman entered the room, Artor stirred.

"You were with Merlin—" said the king. In the strengthening daylight, Guendivar could see all too clearly how the fever had already begun to burn his flesh away.

Ninive nodded and came to the foot of the bed, looking like a wood spirit in her tattered cape, with leaves still caught in her hair.

"We were in the Forest of Caledon. He wanted to come to you—"

"But something happened. He touched me during the battle. What did he do?" the king asked harshly.

"Age came on him suddenly, as it does, in the wild . . ." Ninive said with difficulty. "He used the last of his strength to make a great magic. And when it was over I felt him all around me, as if he had not gone away, but become present everywhere in the world."

"Perhaps it must be so," Artor murmured then. "It was ever the way for the prophet to go before the king. . . ."

Later that morning, when the king had slipped once more into uneasy sleep, Guendivar consented to walk out into the sunlight and take a little food. They had set up a rude table and there was some thin ale and barley bread and hard cheese. Presently, she was joined by Ninive and Morgause.

"How bad is the king's wound?" asked the girl.

Guendivar fixed her eyes on the broken gate, through which she could see the edge of the bluff and the gleam of river beyond, as if she could bear to hear the answer but not to read it in the older woman's eyes.

"Bad enough, if the blade has only penetrated the layers of muscle that sheathe the belly. But if it opened the gut . . ." Morgause shook her head. "There is nothing I can do."

Guendivar turned. "You are the Lady of the Lake! We must take him there," she said desperately. "The Cauldron healed him before!"

Morgause stared at her as if, sunk in her own sorrow, she had forgotten who she was.

"Could he endure the jolting of a horselitter for so long?" asked Ninive, looking from one to the other.

"He will die if he stays here," Morgause said slowly. "Perhaps, if a coracle would float this far upstream, we could take him by water part of the way."

"We will do it!" Guendivar stood up suddenly. "I am the Tiernissa, and even Betiver will obey!"

"You are the Tiernissa, queen in the realm of men," said Morgause, something kindling in her face that had not been there before, "as I am the Hidden Queen, the White Raven who reigns in the country of the soul."

"Among my mother's people I might be counted a queen as well," said Ninive, "though the forest is where I rule."

"With three queens to care for him, surely Artor will be healed!" exclaimed Guendivar, and in that moment, when the sun shone so brightly on the hills, she could even believe it true.

As the coracle began its journey downriver, Morgause saw two ravens lift from the old thorn tree and fly away before them. On the next day, there were a dozen, and after that, always at least that many, circling the boat and flying ahead or behind it.

Guendivar would stiffen when she saw them, as if to defend the king, though the birds showed no signs of hunger. The warriors who paced them along the bank had another interpretation, and said that Lugos and the Lady of Battles had sent their birds to guard their champion. Ninive said it was Woden, who had given Merlin his Spear.

But Morgause remembered how Artor had found the head of Brannos in the White Mount at Londinium, and claimed the old king's place as Guardian of Britannia. It was said that the ravens had come to him that day, recognizing their chieftain. Perhaps it was the ravens of Brannos that followed Artor now, but whether they escorted him to death or to greater glory she could not tell.

At first some of the men waded with the coracle as it floated down the river, easing it over the shallows and clearing obstructions. But presently the water became deeper, and needed only an occasional dip of the boatman's paddle to keep the king moving smoothly towards Luguvalium. Always, while the other two rode with the warriors, one of the queens sat with him, singing, and laying cloths cooled by the waters of the river upon his burning brow.

Morgause could sense Artor's pain even when she was not beside him. The infusions of white willow she gave him did little to dull it. She had fed him a stew of leeks and caught their scent from the wound. She was sure now that there was a perforation there, and putrefaction in the belly, and when delirium set him babbling of old battles she was almost glad.

Before the Cam reached the Salmaes firth, they turned aside into the river that flowed north from Voreda, and moved upstream, towing the coracle where necessary by ropes pulled by men on the shore. Each night was just a little longer, and it seemed that the king's strength ebbed with the lessening of the sun's power. He was still fighting—she thought sometimes that was why he so often dreamed of war—but more and more often, consciousness fled entirely to give his tortured body a few hours of uneasy rest.

When they came at last to Voreda, they paused to construct a horselitter, and began the final part of the journey into the hills.

Morgause took a deep breath. Always, in the great hills, there was a living silence, a mingling of wind in leaves and the voice of waterfalls, or perhaps it was the breathing of the mountains themselves that she heard. Overhead, a raven rested on the wind. They had halted in the shade of a stand of birches to breathe the horses just before the last rise, and in the quiet, that hush filled her awareness.

The heavy warmth of the lowlands had sapped strength of mind and body, but Morgause felt new vigor flowing into her with every step she took into the hills. As she walked back along the line to check on Artor, it seemed to her that surely he must be the better for it as well. And indeed, she found him awake, staring around him with fever-bright eyes.

"Where are we?" he whispered.

"We are just below the circle of stones on the brow of the hill."

The king nodded. "I remember."

"Beyond the next turning the trail runs downward. Soon we will see before us the Lake and the Island."

"I do not think I will ever come there—" said Artor with a sigh.

Morgause took his wrist, and felt the pulse flicker like a guttering candle flame. Guendivar and Ninive had dismounted as well, and seeing them talking, came to join her.

"What is it?" asked Guendiver, bending to smooth the sweat-soaked hair back from Artor's brow. "Is there more pain?" Morgause could hear the effort it took to keep her voice even.

"Oh, my beloved," he breathed, "it is beyond pain. The sinews of my being are withering, and each step frays them further. I cannot go on. . . ."

"My king," Betiver said desperately, "we are almost to the Lake!"

Ninive took Morgause's arm. "Lady, let him wait in the circle; perhaps he will draw some strength from its power. Cannot we run ahead and bring the Cauldron here?"

Ninive had been a priestess at the Lake, thought Morgause. She was her granddaughter, heir to her power—perhaps the Goddess spoke through her now.

"The circle of stones . . ." echoed Artor. "I can feel it calling. Sister, if you have forgiven me for the wrong I did you by my birth, let me rest there. . . ."

"My brother," she asked, "can you find it in your heart to forgive *me*?"

He shook his head a little. "Our son's blood cancelled all debts, Morgause."

"I will go," she said softly, though her voice shook. "Wait for me, Artor! Wait for me!"

As she started down the trail, she heard his whisper behind her— "I will . . . if I can. . . ."

Artor lay upon the breast of the mountain, embraced by the open sky. He could sense the strength of the stones like a royal guard, he himself at their center, and the hill on which they stood surrounded by mountains, and this land of lake and mountain itself the still center of the circles of the world.

They had wished to build a shade above him, but he would not have it. He needed the light. He breathed more easily here than he had in days, but he had no illusions about his condition. From time to time the dark shape of a raven moved across his field of vision. *Soon,* he thought, *I will come with you. Be patient for just a little while.*

In his lucid moments it had gradually come to him that his disintegration had progressed too far for even the Cauldron to heal. Its power was to restore the natural order, and Nature's way, for a body so wasted as his, was to let the spirit go.

The kingdom he had ruled from Camalot was ended, and who would guard Britannia now? He twitched restlessly, remembering the young foxes of Medraut's prophecy. What would come to the land if one of them should try to set himself above the others, brandishing the Chalybe sword? Even the priestesses of the Isle could not guard it against a determined attacker—

He must have moaned, because suddenly Betiver was leaning over him. "My lord, do you need water?"

Artor swallowed. "The Sword—bring it here. . . ." He closed his eyes for a moment, until he felt the familiar ridges of the hilt beneath his hand. He tried to grip it, amazed at how little strength remained in his fingers. But even that was enough for him to feel the current of power.

Defender . . . he prayed, *what is Your will for this blade?* and, in the next moment, trembled beneath a flood of images as he understood what he must do.

Guendivar's hands were cool upon his face, lifting him, and he felt a little water from the skin bag dribble across dry lips. He looked up at Betiver.

"Take the Sword down to the Lake's edge, and with all the power that is in you, throw it in."

"Artor! It is the strength of the kingdom!" exclaimed Betiver.

"It is—it will always be—so long as it does not fall into evil hands! Take it and go, and tell me what befalls!"

When Betiver had departed, Artor lay back again, waiting for his racing pulse to slow. His frame seemed hardly solid enough to keep the gallop of his heart from carrying him away. His body was an empty vessel being filled by the sunlight, or perhaps it was the fever that was burning away his mortality as the dross is burned when the Goddess puts on her smith's apron and purifies the ore in the fire.

Artor's skin is so transparent, thought Guendivar, *he is like a vessel filled with light.* . . . She had always known him as strong and, in his way, attractive; now, with flesh wasted to reveal the pure line of bone, he was beautiful. *And I am going to lose him.* Her stomach churned with the ripple of fear that had become all too familiar since the battle on the Cam.

He seemed to be sleeping, but she could not be sure. Through the link that had grown between them since Beltain, she sensed that for much of the time he lived in the dim borderland between sleep and waking—or perhaps it was the borders of the Otherworld. She had talked to him often on this journey, not knowing whether he could hear her, but there was still so much to say.

"I have missed so much," she said in a low voice. "Children, and the comfort of your arms through the long years. I weep because I could not give you a true son to carry that sword after you were gone. But to no other woman was this blessing given, to rule beside you as your queen. And if the kingdom we tried to build must fall, still, we tried, and for a little while at least we kept back the dark."

Gently she stroked his hair. "If you must leave me, I think I will go south again, to Afallon. Would you like to come with me, my love, so that one day we may lie together upon the holy isle?"

She heard a footstep, and looked up as Betiver came up the hill. He was empty-handed, and she frowned. Had so much time passed?

"And see, here is Betiver back again," she said then, and Artor opened his eyes, so perhaps he had been listening after all.

"Is it done?" asked the king. "What did you see?"

Betiver was staring at the grass. A muscle jumped in his jaw. "The wind on the water, and a splash. What more could there be?"

"The Sword going into the Lake!" said Artor with a

strength that made everyone turn to see. "For you have not done what I asked! Go once more, Betiver, and obey my command, if I am still your king."

Ravens rose in a black cloud, carking with angry voices as Betiver started back down the hill. Several flapped after him, winged shadows of Artor's will.

Guendivar and the warriors sat in silence, waiting for his return. And yet the time seemed still too short for a man to have climbed down to the Lake and back when Betiver came again.

"Betiver, I trusted you!" The king's voice thinned with sorrow. "For five and twenty years you have been with me, closer than kin! Will even you betray me at the end?"

Betiver stretched out his hands, his cheeks glistening with tears. "My lord, wait for them to bring the Cauldron, and heal you, and take the Sword back again! Or if you must leave us, do not deprive us of the only hope we will have! You have named no successor! How shall we choose a true king, if not by the Sword?"

"You are all my heirs!" the king said strongly. "Everyone who hears my story! And it is not by arms that the heritage I leave you shall be defended...." Artor's head moved weakly against the pillow. "You must find hope in your hearts, not in the Sword...." He tried to speak again and coughed. Guendivar saw he did not have the strength for more.

"Betiver," she said with the steel she had learned in ten years as regent for the king, "I command you to do Artor's will, in the name of the love you bear for me...." His eyes lifted to hers, and she saw the desperation go out of them, replaced by a grief as deep as her own.

"Lady," he answered in a breaking voice, "my son also lies among the dead on Camboglanna's field."

His steps were slow as he started down the hill towards the Lake once more.

Morgause sat in the bow of the boat, swaying as Nest poled them towards the shore. The Cauldron was cradled in her arms. Ninive crouched before her, holding the bag that held the medicines and other gear it had taken them all this while to find, for they might have to spend some time on the hill before Artor could be moved again.

We have the time . . . Morgause affirmed silently, turning on her seat to gaze up the hill. *He is safe in the circle. He will live till I return.* . . .

Beneath its wrappings the Cauldron quivered against her belly, as if she held something living. For so many years she had desired it and, seizing it, had herself been possessed and transformed by its power. But for more than a dozen years she had served as its priestess, handling it only with the prescribed and warded touch of ritual. This intimate contact dizzied her.

Brigantia be with me, she prayed. *Let me work Thy will!*

A movement on the shore caught her eye and she leaned forward, staring. "Nest, turn the boat," she commanded suddenly. "Toward the little beach by the boulder."

Betiver stood at the water's edge, holding the Sword. Even from here she could see that he was weeping.

"What are you doing?" she cried. "Is Artor—"

"Oh, Lady, he commanded me to throw it in!" Betiver called back, his face working.

The boat rocked as Morgause stood up. Before Artor, the women of her blood had been the Sword's keepers.

"Stop! You must not—" she began, but Betiver was already drawing back the blade, whirling it up and around behind him.

For a moment, at the height of his swing, the Sword seemed to hover, blazing in the light of the sun. Then it flew free, soaring above the water in an arc of flame. Morgause lurched forward, felt Ninive clutch at her legs at the same moment as the Cauldron leaped from fingers that no longer had the power to hold it.

The Cauldron spun across the water like a silver wheel, the Sword drove downward. Where they met, Light flared outward, blinding the senses. But as Morgause fell back, it was not the afterimage of Sword and Cauldron that remained imprinted behind her eyelids, but that of a goddess, reaching up from the waters of the Lake to embrace the god. . . .

* * *

Artor jerked back to consciousness, gasping. *I am dying!* he thought, but his pain-wracked body still imprisoned him. It was the world that was whirling, to settle at last into a new configuration, and he understood that the perfect balance for which he had been striving since first he drew the Sword from the Stone was at last attained.

"Guendivar!" He reached out to her. "Do you feel it? It is done!"

She caught his hand against her breast, and he felt her heart beating almost as wildly as his own. He grinned as a warrior does at the end of a battle fought past the borders of desperation, and beyond hope, won. In her face he saw a reflected wonder.

"Help me to move—" he said with sudden authority. "Set me with my back against a stone."

The queen nodded, and men came to lift him, grim understanding in their eyes. They set him against one of the boulders that marked out a rectangle at the eastern edge of the circle, its face worn smooth by the centuries. It made a royal seat, he thought, for the death of a king.

Artor took a deep breath, and let it slowly out. The cold stone warmed against him; a vibration travelled down his spine and into the depths of the earth, then fountained upward. And now he could hear it—the stones were singing, crying out in recognition of his sovereignty. Could not the others hear? He coughed, and coughed again, feeling the bonds that held soul to body fray.

Guendivar knelt beside him, weeping.

"My love . . . my love . . ." he whispered, understanding now so many things. "We cannot lose each other. I will never be far away from you. When my body sleeps in the earth, my spirit will watch over Britannia. . . . Watch with me, my queen, until we are joined once more. . . ."

She took his hand, and Artor smiled. He was aware of voices—Betiver and Morgause and Ninive, panting from their swift climb, but he could not find the strength to speak to them. He let his eyes close.

Through his eyelids he could still see sunlight; his other

senses seemed to sharpen. The borders of his body could no longer hold him; awareness expanded outward through earth and air and water. Beyond the surfaces he had always accepted as reality, he perceived the real Britannia, the true country of the heart that no matter what evils passed in the world of men would always endure. This was his kingdom. Why, he wondered, had it taken him so long to understand?

To Guendivar, the light that had filled Artor's face seemed slowly to fade. But the radiance all around her was growing. Blinking back tears, she looked up from the emptied body, wondering where he had gone.

From Morgause came an anguished cry, and as if that had been a signal, the ravens rushed upward in a glistening dark cloud. Three times above the still body the black birds circled, calling out in grief and triumph. Then from their midst Guendivar saw one Raven rise and wing southward, its feathers turning incandescent in the sun.

REX AEТERПUS

A·D· 1189

"T HEY SAY THAT YOU KNOW ALL THE BRETON TALES," SAYS the king. "Can you sing of King Arthur as well?" He taps a leather-bound book on the table before him. "Here are the *Lais* of Marie, that she dedicated to me. I have read the *Brut* also, and Geoffrey's *Historia*, when I was a young man. And I have heard very many songs of the jongleurs of your country. You will be hard put, I warn you, to find anything that I have not heard!"

The bard inclines his head. He is old, but seems strong, with a pair of dark eyes beneath bushy brows. He is a very big man.

"Lord king, I know many tales that no one has heard, of Artor, and other things." In the light from the pointed window, his beard glints silver against the dusty white of his robe.

"Hah!" says King Henry. "Sit, then, for I've a fox that gnaws my vitals, and a good tale may help me to forget the pain." He has filled the castle of Chinon with beautiful things. The stool to which he gestures the bard has a seat of red leather and feet carved like griffons' claws.

"That was how King Arthur died," says the bard. "Stabbed

183

in the belly by his son." He speaks the French tongue with the deep music of the Celtic lands.

The king gives him a sharp look. "My sons have done the same, both Richard, who fights me, and John, who intrigues with that viper Philippe Auguste while smiling and praising my name. But you surprise me," he goes on, sipping more wine. "Mostly the Bretons say that Arthur never died, but sleeps in the Western Isles, or in a cavern in the hills, or in the vale of Avalon. The Welshmen, too, especially when they are preaching rebellion."

"Those who speak of Avalon come closest to the truth," rumbles the bard. "He is buried there."

"Now how did that come to pass?" Henry pulls his robe more closely around him and leans back in his carved chair, one eyebrow raised.

"The battle of Camlann was fought in the north of Angleterre, near the Wall," says the bard, "not in Cornuailles, as so many say. And when Arthur was dead, his body was carried south by Queen Guenivere and buried in Inis Witrin, which is the Isle of Avalon."

"Indeed?" The king cocks his head, willing to be amused. "Say then, if you know so much, what manner of man was Arthur, and how old he was when he met his end?"

"A big man, like you, and fifty-five years of age when he died. He too quarreled with churchmen for the good of the land, and dreamed of an empire in Gaul."

Henry frowns. "I have passed him, then, for I am fifty-six. I wonder, do you mean to threaten or to flatter me?"

The bard shrugs. "Arthur walked the earth, and loved greatly, and strove greatly to make good laws and keep the peace and preserve the land from her enemies."

"So also have I," the king replies, more softly. "But you take the magic from the story, telling it so!"

"Is it not a greater wonder that this same history should still be recounted some six centuries after Arthur died, and in every country of Christendom?" the bard answers more softly still.

King Henry shakes his head, laughing. "You will never make your fortune telling such tales to mortal kings! We prefer to believe that Arthur lived in an age of marvels, and avoid comparisons!"

"But what if it were true?"

"If it could be proved, you mean?" Suddenly the king grasps his sinewy arm. "Who are you, to know such things?"

For a moment the bard considers him. Then, very gently, he smiles, and Henry finds his grip loosening. "I have been called by many names. I am a Wild Man in the wood, and a bard in the courts of kings. I am a wanderer upon the roads of the world, and the prophet of Arthur. And you yourself can prove the truth of my words—"

He leans forward. "The abbey at Glastonbury burned five years ago, and the monks are still rebuilding. Command them to dig deep between the two pyramids in the churchyard. They will find there a coffin hollowed from a log of oak, and in it the bones of Arthur, and at his feet, Guenivere, with a leaden cross that gives their names."

"That would settle the Welsh!" exclaims the king, then sobers. "They claim Arthur as their Defender, but so do the English, and we Normans likewise, for my grandson bears his name. These days, he belongs to everyone. Why is that, do you suppose?" Henry says then. "Why should he matter so?"

"Because he loved Britannia . . ." answers the bard. "Because for a little while he kept her safe against the dark." He sits back, considering the king.

"I tell you these things so that you may know that such deeds can be achieved by mortal men. And yet what the Welsh and the Bretons tell you is the truth as well. Arthur's spirit never departed—neither to Heaven nor to the Otherworld. He watches over the Hallowed Isle. . . ."

PEOPLE AПD PLACES

A note on pronunciation:

British names are given in fifth-century spelling, which does not yet reflect pronunciation changes. Initial letters should be pronounced as they are in English. Medial letters are as follows:

SPELLED	PRONOUNCED
p	b
t	d
k/c	(soft) g
b	v (approximately)
d	soft "th" (modern Welsh "dd")
g	"yuh"
m	v
ue	w

†
PEOPLE

CAPITALS = major character
* = historical personnage
( ) = dead before story begins
[ ] = name as given in later literature
Italics = diety or mythological personnage

*Aelle—king of the South Saxons
Aggarban [Agravaine]—third son of Morgause
*Agricola—prince of Demetia
*Alaric II—king of the Visigoths
(*Ambrosius Aurelianus—emperor of Britannia and Vitalinus' rival)
(*Amlodius—Artor's grandfather)
Amminius—one of Artor's men
ARTOR [Arthur]—son of Uthir and Igierne, high king of Britannia
(Artoria Argantel—Artor's grandmother)
Beowulf—king of the Geats in Denmark
BETIVER [Bedivere]—nephew to Riothamus, one of Artor's Companions
Bleitisbluth—a Pictish chieftain
Brigantia/Brigid—British goddess of healing, inspiration, and the land
*Budic—a grandson of Riothamus, lord of Civitas Aquilonia
CAI—son of Caius Turpilius, Artor's foster-brother and Companion
*Caninus [Aurelius Caninus]—son of the prince of Glevum, ally of Medraut
CATAUR [Cador]—prince of Dumnonia
Cathubodva—Lady of Ravens, a British war goddess
*Ceawlin—son of Cynric and grandson of Ceretic
Ceincair—a priestess on the Isle of Maidens

(*Ceretic [Cerdic]—king of the West Saxons)
*Chlodovechus [Clovis]—king of the Franks in Gallia
*Chlotild—queen of the Franks
*Conan—lord of Venetorum
*Constantine—son of Cataur, prince of Dumnonia
*Creoda—son of Icel of Anglia
*Cuil—a brigand
*Cunobelinus—warleader of the northern Votadini
*Cunoglassus—a prince of Guenet, ally of Medraut
Cunovinda—a young priestess on the Isle of Maidens
*Cymen—Aelle's eldest son
*Cynric—son of Ceretic, king of the West Saxons
*Daniel Dremrud—son of Riothamus
Doli—a Pictish warrior in the service of Morgause
*Drest Gurthinmoch—high king of the Picts
(*Dubricius—bishop of Isca and head of the church in Britannia)
*Dumnoval [Dyfnwal]—lord of the Southern Votadini
Edrit—a young warrior in the service of Aggarban
Eldaul the younger [Eldol]—prince of Glevum
*Eormenric—son of Oesc, child-king of Cantuware
*Feragussos [Fergus]—king of the Scotti of Dal Riada
*Gipp—Norse founder of Gippewic in Essex, Medraut's ally
GORIAT [Gareth]—fourth son of Morgause
(Gorlosius [Gorlois]—first husband of Igierne, father of Morgause)
Gracilia—wife of Gualchmai
GUALCHMAI [Gawain]—first son of Morgause
GUENDIVAR [Gwenivere]—Artor's queen
*Guenomarcus—lord of Plebs Legionorum
Gwyhir [Gaheris]—second son of Morgause
Hæthwæge—a Saxon wisewoman
(*Hengest—king of Cantuware, leader of Saxon revolt)
*Henry II—king of England
*Icel—king of the Anglians in Britannia
IGIERNE [Igraine]—Artor's mother, Lady of the Lake

Johannes Rutilius—brother-in-law to Riothamus, Betiver's father

Julia—a nun from the Isle of Glass, Guendivar's companion

(Kea—a British slave girl among the Picts, Medraut's first woman)

Father Kedi—an Irish priest at the court of Artor

Leodegranus [Leodegrance]—prince of Lindinis, Guendivar's father

(Leudonus [Lot]—king of the Votadini)

Maglouen [Maelgwn]—a prince of Guenet, Medraut's ally

(*Magnus Maximus [Maxen Wledig]—general serving in Britain who was proclaimed emperor 383–388)

Marcus Conomorus [Mark of Cornwall]—son of Constantine

Martinus of Viroconium—an ally of Medraut

Maxentius—a grandson of Riothamus

MEDRAUT—fifth son of Morgause, by Artor

Melwas [Meleagrance]—an Irishman born in Guenet, abductor of Guendivar

MERLIN—druid and wizard, Artor's advisor

Morcant Bulc—heir to Dun Breatann

MORGAUSE—daughter of Igierne and Gorlosius, queen of the Votadini

(*Naitan Morbet—king of all the provinces of the Picts)

Nest—a priestess on the Isle of Maidens

Ninive—daughter of Gualchmai by a woman of the hills

(*Oesc—grandson of Hengest and king of Cantuware, Eormenric's father)

*Othar, Ela, Adgils, Admund [Othere, Onela, Eadgils, Eadmund]—King Ottar of Sweden, his brother Ali, his sons Adils and Eadmund

Paulinus Clutorix—lord of Viroconium

*Peretur [Peredur]—son of Eleutherius, lord of Eboracum

*Pompeius Regalis [Riwal]—lord of Domnonia

*Ridarchus—king at Alta Cluta and protector of Luguvalium

Rigana—widow of Oesc, Eormenric's mother

*Riothamus—ruler of Armorica

*Theodoric—a Gothic admiral in the service of Britannia

*Theuderich—king of the Franks, son of Chlodovechus and a
   concubine and one of his successors, along with Chlo-
   domer, Childebert, and Lothar (by Queen Clotild)
Uorepona—the "Great Mare," high queen of the Picts
(Uthir [Uther Pendragon]—Artor's father)
Verica—a young priestess on the Isle of Maidens
(*Vitalinus, the Vor-Tigernus—ruler of Britannia who brought
   in the Saxons)
*Vortipor—son of Agricola, prince of Demetia

†

PLACES

Afallon [Avalon]—Isle of Apples, Glastonbury
Alba—Scotland
Altaclutha—kingdom of the Clyde
Ambrosiacum—Amesbury
Anglia—Lindsey and Lincoln
Annuen [Annwyn]—the land of the dead
Aquae Sulis—Bath
Armorica—Britanny
Belisama fluvius—River Ribble, Lancashire
Bodotria aestuarius—Firth of Forth
Britannia—Great Britain
Caellwic—Kelliwic, Cornwall
Caledonian forest—southern Scotland
Calleva—Silchester
Camalot [Camelot]—Cadbury Castle, Somerset
Camboglanna [Camlann]—fortress of Birdoswald, the Wall
Camulodunum—Colchester
Cantium, Cantuware—Kent
Castra Legionis—Caerleon
Cendtire—Kintyre peninsula
Civitas Aquilonia—Quimper, Brittany

Clutha—River Clyde
Demetia—Pembroke and Carmarthen
Domnonia—Cotes du Nord, Brittany
Dumnonia—Cornwall and Devon
Dun Bara—Barry Hill, Perth
Dun Breatann—"fortress of the Britons," Dumbarton Rock
Dun Eidyn—Edinburgh Rock
Durnovaria—Dorchester, Dorset
Durobrivae—1. Rochester, Kent; 2. Water Newton, Cambridge
Fodreu—Fortriu, Fife
Forest of Caledon—Caledonian forest, southern Scotland
Gallia—France
Giants' Dance—Stonehenge
Gippewic—in Essex
Glevum—Gloucester
Guenet [Gwynedd]—Denbigh and Caernarvon
Isca (Silurum)—Caerwent
Isle of Glass (Inis Witrin)—Glastonbury
Isle of Maidens in the Lake—Derwentwater, Cumbria
Lindinis—Ilchester, Somerset
Lindum—Lincoln
Londinium—London
Metaris aestuarius—the Wash
Mona—Anglesey
Plebs Legionorum—St. Pol de Léon, Brittany
Pyrenaei montes—the Pyrenees
Sabrina fluvia—the Severn River and estuary
Segontium—Caernarvon, Wales
Sorviodunum—Salisbury
Summer Country—Somerset
Tava—River Tay
Tolosa—Toulouse
Urbs Legionis (Deva)—Chester
Uxela fluvius—River Axe, Severn estuary
Venetorum—Vannes, in Brittany

Venta Belgarum—Winchester
Venta Siluricum—Caerwent, Wales
Viroconium—Wroxeter
Voreda—Old Penrith, Cumberland

DISCOVER THE KINGDOM OF KING ARTHUR
by award-winning author
DIANA L. PAXSON

THE HALLOWED ISLE BOOK ONE:
THE BOOK OF THE SWORD
78870-5 / $10.00 US / $14.50 Can

THE HALLOWED ISLE BOOK TWO:
THE BOOK OF THE SPEAR
80546-4 / $10.00 US / $14.50 Can

THE HALLOWED ISLE BOOK THREE:
THE BOOK OF THE CAULDRON
80547-2 / $10.00 US / $14.50 Can

THE HALLOWED ISLE BOOK FOUR:
THE BOOK OF THE STONE
80548-0 / $11.00 US / $16.50 Can

Printed in the United States
58107LVS00002B/128

9 780380 805488